# The Arena's Call

## Book 4 of Adventures on Brad

by

## Tao Wong

# Copyright

The Arena's Call
Copyright © 2020 Tao Wong. All rights reserved.
Copyright © 2020 Felipe deBarros Cover Artist
Copyright © 2020 Sarah Anderson Cover Designer

A Starlit Publishing Book
Published by Starlit Publishing
69 Teslin Rd
Whitehorse, YT
Y1A 3M5
Canada

www.starlitpublishing.com

Ebook ISBN: 9781775380955
Paperback ISBN: 9781989458792

# Books in the Adventures on Brad series

# Contents

# Chapter 1

Separated from the trio of heroes by a simple metal gate, the twelve-foot-long, luminescent green scaled and squat drake lay dozing in the Mana-lit cavern. Enclosed all around by cold stone, the drake slumbered fitfully, the silence only broken by the slow drip of water that formed a pool in the corner. As the trio watched, the drake yawned lazily and showed the inside of its pink mouth, one filled with rows upon rows of sharp, deadly teeth.

"I am not enjoying these surprises," Omrak said softly while the trio edged backwards from the metal gate. Reaching over his broad shoulders, the giant blond Northerner pulled his large two-handed sword from its utilitarian sheath to eye the blade.

"Well, it's just a single Dungeon Champion," Daniel Chai said as he adjusted his shield. His plate mail armor clanking slightly as he moved, the shorter, slant-eyed and flat-nosed Adventurer added, "I rather like the change after fighting all those lizards."

"Tough," Asin hissed, her furry tail lashing out beside her as cat ears twitched, clawed hands kneading the soil as she watched behind them. Her short cloak covered her body, helping her to hide in the shadows she'd instinctively found, her dark fur blending in.

"I agree with Hero Asin," Omrak growled. "A drake is significantly tougher than what we have dealt with before."

"Too tough for us?" Daniel asked, eyes narrowing even further to slits. While no longer a Beginner Adventurer, Daniel knew he was still new to the adventuring lifestyle. It had not even been two years since he left his lifestyle as a Miner.

"For us heroes? Nay. We should be able to defeat this opponent," Omrak said with renewed confidence. The teenager flashed a grin, lazily swinging the sword around his hand as he limbered up. "I but spoke for caution, to temper overconfidence. A hero must understand themselves."

Asin chuffed slightly, her back arching and tail straightening for a second as her cat ears tilted downward. Daniel coughed at the same time as he stopped the bubbling laughter. Omrak telling them to not be overconfident. Daniel found himself smiling, the spike of concern fading.

"Start," Asin said and walked over to the wooden lever that controlled the gate. She regarded her friends one last time to receive their agreement before she pulled on the device. Daniel shifted forward, his heavy crossbow in hand, a bulbous bolt locked in place.

With a screech, the pulley rose to the clanking of chains. As the noise reverberated around the cavern, the drake woke from its sleep. Twisting its long, sinuous neck towards the source of the noise, it hissed at Omrak who was in the process of ducking underneath the rising blockade.

"Come. Let us do battle and determine our worthiness!" Omrak roared his challenge and kept the monster's attention as he strode in, his simple, black leather breastplate made of monster hide the Northerner's only protection. In retaliation, the drake roared back its challenge.

"Good," whispered Daniel, the crossbow snug against his shoulder as he crouched. He gently squeezed the trigger, the crossbow kicking back as he targeted the monster's open mouth. Not realising he was doing it, Daniel held his breath as the bolt spun through the air and missed the open mouth, slamming into the creature's neck. A small explosion resulted as the explosive bolt triggered, tearing off scales and making the monster scream again.

"Missed!" Asin laughed, lobbing a knife underhand. The knife glowed as it flew through the air as Asin activated **Piercing Shot**, allowing the throwing knife to drill into the drake's mouth. The monster roared, the pain making the creature thrash. Its long tail swung around, careening like the end of a catapult into Omrak who had charged forwards to close the distance.

Omrak snarled as he blocked the attack, sword held at an angle as the tail impacted against the weapon and his body. The giant Northerner's feet skidded backwards, digging into the ground and throwing up soil before the monster's momentum finally came to an end. Omrak's sword glowed slightly under his Skill, the drake's tail notched from the blocked blow, scales crushed and blood beginning to fall. Taking advantage of the momentarily slowed appendage, Asin bounded up the creature's body before flinging herself high into the air. Knives held beneath her, she landed with a thump on the monster's back. Rearing itself backward in pain, the drake roared once more in an attempt to throw the Catkin off, even as she wrapped her feet around its body.

"What was that?" Daniel shouted as he rushed forwards, his crossbow discarded as he drew his enchanted hammer and shield. As the drake swung its head towards Daniel, he skidded and fought for purchase on loose sand and slick stone.

Asin ignored her partner's incredulous shout, too busy attempting to lever a scale off the monster's back. Even as she did so, arcs of electricity danced from her body into the drake's, the enchanted bracers she wore continually pulling electricity from the environment and her aura and grounding it in her foe's body.

Omrak snarled, swinging his great sword with both hands as he struck the drake. Anger coursing through his body at being ignored for his friends, the Northerner swung, again and again, trading ferocity for skill. Even as he righted himself from a stumble, he overextended and was forced to throw himself down to escape a grasping claw.

Struggling to his feet and running forwards, Daniel focused and triggered his skill **Shield Bash.** The attack slammed the monster's lunging jaws

11

into the air as he pushed forth with his feet. With quick steps, Daniel swung the spike on his hammer into the exposed wound in the drake's neck as the head retracted from the initial attack. The spike sunk nearly all the way to the hilt before being ripped out, followed shortly by a flood of blood.

The drake hissed in pain and swung its head at Daniel. This time, Daniel was unable to block it in time, the blow sending him skidding across the ground before ending at the wall. Lying on the ground, Daniel groaned, grateful that the plate armour he wore absorbed the majority of the impact. He focused for a second, casting a **Healer's Mark** on his body, starting the healing process to deal with the incipient bruises and pulled muscles.

"Nay, your battle is with me!" roared Omrak as the drake attempted to rush Daniel. His shout triggered his ability **Challenge of the North**, drawing the drake's unwilling form to attack him again. Head lowered, it swiped with its front claw only to be blocked by Omrak's great sword.

Grinning, Daniel stood up and adjusted his helmet before he took off running, listening to Omrak's continued taunts and Asin's yowling as her enchantments took their toll on the monster's body. *Time to finish this*, Daniel thought.

\*\*\*

As the drake let loose one last roar and collapsed almost on Omrak, Daniel exhaled with relief. As Asin tried to sit up from the floor, Daniel pushed her back down with one hand.

"Lie down damnit!" Daniel growled. "I've got to set your hip first unless you want it to heal crooked."

"Hurts!" Asin yowled but complied, her claws kneading the loose sand as she focused on the large Dungeon Champion's corpse. The Champion glowed for a moment, its body breaking apart as the Mana that held it together dispersed. With a light tinkle, the blue-grey Mana stone dropped to the ground, almost making Asin sit up again. Only a flash of pain as Daniel set her hip stopped her.

"Ah, here's the chest!" Omrak happily tromped over to the chest and on Asin's gold-filled heart. With a careless heave, Omrak opened the chest, curiosity driving his actions. Too late, Daniel

13

noticed the Northerner's carelessness as the chest released a cloud of gas into Omrak's face. Coughing and wiping at his face, Omrak staggered back.

"Idiot. You're supposed to check first!" Daniel snarled as he finished casting **Minor Healing (II)** on Asin before he strode over to Omrak. "Hold still." With deft movements, Daniel gripped the Northerner by his leather tunic and splashed water over the man's face.

"Hero Daniel. I cannot see." Omrak said, his voice higher than normal, almost panicked.

"It's fine. Just hold still," Daniel said soothingly. One hand shifted to grip the blond giant's arm, the skin contact required for Daniel to trigger his Gift. That was what society called it – a Gift – but for those individuals like Daniel, born with an unexplained power, it was often a burden - for every Gift had a price.

As Daniel extended his Gift into Omrak's body, a flood of information flowed into his mind. The slightly pulled hamstring. The twisted ankle. The bunion that was growing on Omrak's foot. The poison that had invaded Omrak's eyes, blocking the nerves that gave sight. All this and

14

more swept into Daniel's consciousness. It only took a gentle nudge, the slightest exertion of power to begin the cleansing process. And all it cost Daniel was a memory, a moment of his life. Daniel once again felt it slip from his mind, like an eel from a child's hand.

"Now, come here," Daniel guided Omrak to the wall and sat the man down gently. "Your sight will return in a little while. Till then, sit and think about what you did, you big lunk."

"My apologies, Hero Daniel," Omrak rumbled, bobbing his head in shame.

"No traps," Asin announced behind the pair triumphantly, having taken the time to review the once trapped chest. The Catkin then reached inside and fished out a single item - a curved knife in a sheath. On closer inspection, the group noticed runes that indicated that the weapon was likely enchanted.

"Only one?" Daniel said, disappointment tingeing his voice. After all, Karlak had given them two items in the final chest.

"One." Asin nodded, ears pointed downwards slightly, her tail drooping.

"What! Is there only one treasure?" Omrak shouted as he pushed himself to his feet, hands waving around in front of him.

"Sit down," Daniel snapped at Omrak. "And yes, there's only one."

"Do you think the trap destroyed the other?" Omrak asked guiltily.

"No," Asin said snippily before she walked over to the Northerner and lifted the Mana stone from his pouch.

"What...? Is that you, Asin?" Omrak said, patting at his newly emptied pouch. "Wait! You only took the stone, right? Asin?"

"She's gone," Daniel sighed, shaking his head. Thankfully the Peel Dungeon had an exit from the Dungeon Champion's cavern. It saved the team from having to trek through the previous floors on their way out of the Dungeon after completing it.

"Why did she leave?" Omrak said, frowning as he turned to where Daniel sat. "Did I do something wrong?"

"No. We're just on a timetable. The Guild closes earlier in Peel, remember?" Daniel patiently explained. With nothing better to do, Daniel pulled his hammer out and began the laborious process

16

of cleaning his weapon. As the silence lengthened, broken only by the swish of cloth on metal, Omrak cleared his throat.

"Yes?" Daniel said.

"Can you tell me a story?" Omrak said, flushing slightly.

"A story?" Daniel said.

"Or just speak," Omrak said hurriedly. "It's just, sitting in the dark in the Dungeon…"

"Sorry," Daniel said with shame. Of course, Omrak was feeling somewhat uncertain. They had spent the last five days battling their way down the Peel Dungeon's floors, fighting smart lizard creatures who set traps, ran away and otherwise harried the team. As their vanguard, Omrak had suffered the most from the constant sniping attacks.

"My grandfather once told me this story, about the god Hanna. You know of her?" At Omrak's nod, Daniel continued. "This was long ago. Long before Ba'al broke into Brad, when there were no Dungeons, and the Immortal War had not been fought. It was a more peaceful time when Erlis's children were numerous and lived

17

with her in her silver palace. Now, Hanna was, and still is, mischievous. Rather than stay at home, she would often sneak down to our plane to frolic with the animals.

"On this day, she found a horse whose coat was the purest white but for the blood that marred it and the wounds that the blood originated from. Hanna rushed forwards, grasping the horse by the side and asked it what had happened. A single touch on the wounds and Hanna pulled her hand back, for the wounds were poisoned. Poisoned with a substance that Hanna had never seen before. But Hanna was a god, a minor god perhaps, but a god and so she vowed to cure the horse."

Caught in the story, Daniel forgot to wipe down his hammer. Instead, he was taken back, to a simpler time when it was just him and his grandfather. A time where the ring of pickaxes would resound from the mines, the never-ending creak of wheels as they rolled new ore out. A more peaceful time.

"Hanna brought back herbs that could cure any poison upon touch. Flowers that when crushed and mixed cleansed the body. Spells,

18

chanted under breath, to drive toxins out. But nothing worked, no herb, no flower, no spell worked. In desperation, she searched through the mud and pulled out leeches, setting them upon the wound. These leeches would suck, drink the foul poison of the wounds and fall aside, twitching. And still, the wound festered, the horse slowly dying."

"Surely it did not die?" Omrak said, head tilted to his friend. This was a story he had not heard.

"Patience, friend. The story is not over. When all hope seemed lost, when the beast lay on the ground, Hanna struck upon one last, desperate idea. Holding forth her own arm, she sliced it open with her knife. Her blood fell, mixing with the toxin. Finally, finally, the toxins left the beast, pushed away by Hanna's divine blood. And so, the horse was healed. But another miracle occurred that day. For divine blood mixed with mortal and through Hanna's sacrifice, the horse transformed. For now, on its head, a single horn grew, a facet of the divine."

"A unicorn!" Omrak cried. "Divine creatures, sacred to all."

"Yes, a unicorn," Daniel said with a smile.

"That was a good story," Omrak said with a smile. "And I think I can see again. At least, enough for us to exit."

"Good. I'm glad you liked it," Daniel said with a smile as he walked over to help his friend stand. Together, the pair exited the Dungeon slowly. Yet, Daniel could not help but remember the last part of the story, the part that Omrak had interrupted him from telling. For the toxins, driven away by the divine blood, would pool with the leeches that fell earlier. And together, they would mutate, creating the first demon-born. Creatures that held a Mana stone – the blood of the divine – in their body which gave them form.

\*\*\*

Later that evening, when things had quietened down, Daniel finally had time to check his notification. Lying in bed, he had to smile. Finally! He had finally achieved his tenth Level and gained access to the Adventurer's Special Skill – Inventory. It had only taken grinding through the entirety of the Peel Dungeon, killing the Dungeon

Champion and getting the Dungeon completion reward. Admittedly, he perhaps shouldn't have used his Gift on that child…

With a quick wave of his hand, Daniel allocated his free attribute points and pushed away his thoughts. Done was done. Two to intelligence, one each to the physical attributes. He was still a front-line fighter after all and while Willpower allowed him to push through the pain and fear that could afflict him, what the team needed more was regular healing. It was, partially, what kept them in the game.

Content with his decision, Daniel flicked his hand and pulled up his character screen to review it in detail.

---

Name: Daniel Chai (Advanced Rank Adventurer)

Class: Level 10 Adventurer (33%)

Sub-classes: Level 7 (Miner) (04%)

Human (Male)

---

---

**Statistics**
Life: 296
Stamina: 296
Mana: 217

**Attributes**
Strength: 28
Agility: 25
Constitution: 31
Intelligence: 23
Willpower: 20
Luck: 15

**Skills**
Unarmed Combat: Level 3 (93/100)
Clubs (Novice): Level 4 (37/100)
Archery: Level 2 (88/100)
Shield (Novice): Level 2 (64/100)
Dodge: Level 9 (03/100)
Combat Sense: Level 9 (18/100)
Perception (Novice): Level 1 (06/100)
Mining: Level 7 (78/100)
Healing (Novice): Level 2 (48/100)
Herb Lore: Level 3 (42/100)

Stealth: Level 2 (29/100)
Cooking: Level 4 (13/100)
Singing: Level 2 (14/100)

**Skill Proficiencies**
Double Strike
Shield Bash
Perin's Blow
Find Weakness
Mapping (II)
Inventory (Adventurer Special)

**Spells**
Minor Healing (II)
Healer's Mark (I)

**Gifts**
Martyr's Touch—The caster may heal oneself or others by touch and concentration, sacrificing a portion of his life to do so. Cost varies depending on the extent of the injuries healed.

# Chapter 2

As Peel held no appeal for the band of Adventurers, not since clearing its Beginner Dungeon, the trio moved on. By common agreement, they would repeat Asin and Daniel's initial trip, taking the journey to Silverstone. The large Dungeon City held not one but two Advanced Dungeons – Aramis and Porthos. In Silverstone lay numerous Adventuring Guilds, enchanters and blacksmiths. All that a trio of eager young Adventurers could want.

"This is a very big city," Omrak said, his eyes slightly glazed as he constantly craned his neck from side to side. Three times the size of Karlak, Silverstone was both a major trading hub and a Dungeon City. Built at the confluence of three main roads and further boosted by the nearby Arq river, the city hosted caravans and merchants from all across the country. Even entering the city had been simple, a matter of flashing their Adventurer cards before being let in.

By unspoken consensus, Asin and Daniel took turns guiding the young giant by his elbow around the numerous pedestrians. Walking in the city was not for the faint of heart, even if Silverstone had a working sewage system. After all, pedestrian dangers included too-fast-moving wagons, Workers and Labourers carrying tonnes of cargo on their shoulders, and tamed pets of various ilk. In a city whose economy was driven by the presence of a pair of Dungeons, the use and keeping of war dogs, savage lizards, hunger beetles and other, more exotic, pets was not unexpected.

It was something that Daniel and Asin had only vaguely noticed on their first visit. Now, old hands at the city, they had begun to realise that there was still much that neither had really paid attention to. Up close, the gleaming, clean white image of the city gave way - the white, insulating clay grimy with dirt at shoulder level. Constant application and cleaning spells did little to stop the constant wear of tens of thousands of civilians pressed together, living their lives.

As they walked through the city, Asin was rubbing her nose, distracted by the stench and constant noise. Her expanded senses were under assault once again after the relative silence of the wilderness, forcing the Catkin to readjust. It thus lay to Daniel to take the lead as he guided the group to the inn that they had once stayed. Unfortunately, it soon became clear that residence at the inn, or any other inn, was going to be difficult to achieve.

Time after time, they were ejected from an inn before they could speak, their backpacks and travel-worn appearance a clear indicator of their needs. Finally exasperated and finding a particularly sympathetic older Innkeeper, Daniel leaned over the bar and asked, plaintively, "What tournament?"

"Oh, you poor boy. You didn't know of it?" Erin the Innkeeper tutted. "A month ago, the Adventurer's Guild announced that there would be a tournament held three weeks from now. Artos is scheduled to reopen in three months."

"I have not heard of this Artos," Omrak rumbled softly.

"Well, you're pretty young, so that's no wonder," Erin said. "It was all the rage thirty years ago. And fifty before that. And fifty before. It opens every fifty years you know?"

"But…?" Daniel said with a frown, brows drawn down as he did the math.

"Oh yes, it's a big mystery why the Dungeon's opening now. But all the Mages say it's for sure

27

opening, so we're holding the tournament early. All the Advanced Adventurers were informed!" Erin chirped.

"Not fair," Asin said with a growl, whiskers turning. "Experienced."

"Oh pish-posh. Of course, it's fair," Erin said. "There are three tiers of experience, and everyone gets allocated according to each tier. The Guild has even announced that there will be a total of seven spots this year. That's two spots for Advanced Adventurers just starting out. Like, well, you."

The group quickly traded glances, their interest peaked. This was good news for them. Obviously, if so much fuss was being made about such a location, the rewards had to be good as well. Even if the tournament had created a temporary housing problem as Adventurers from around the country streamed in along with the Merchants, Alchemists, Trainers and other supporting Classes looking to take advantage of the event.

"Are you sure you have no place for us?" Daniel said, doing his best puppy dog impression. Asin let out a low snort, but Erin, falling for the little boy lost charm that Daniel had on older women melted slightly.

"Well, I do have an attic…" Erin hedged.

"We'll take it."

"It's a bit drafty, and it hasn't been cleaned…"

"We'll take it."

"And I don't have bedding…"

"WE'LL TAKE IT!" Omrak roared, his voice accidentally raised too loud. Instead of looking put off, Erin just smiled enthusiastically at the giant blond man.

"Okay, you'll take it. Rent will be one silver a day for each of you," Erin said with a smile as she turned away to get the attic key. "Paid in advance."

The team hissed in unison, the high rates taking their breath way for a second. Most labourers only earned a single silver for their work in a day. But then again, it made sense. The city was packed to the brim, was larger than Karlak, and had two Advanced Dungeons in it. Of course, it was going to be more expensive.

"You coming?" the matronly Innkeeper called out, hand on the stairway bannister as the three Adventurers slowly came to their senses. With a quick shake of their heads, the trio grabbed their bags and followed her up. While the trio had access to the Adventurer's Class Skill 'Inventory', it was still severely limited and could not store all their belongings. At least, not at the level that they had right now.

Hours later, they stood in the newly cleaned attic, their sleeping bags laid out on fresh straw, a small pile of the inn's belongings in one corner and a larger pile of junk near the trapdoor. Asin was in the corner with a newly brought up pot of water, a brush and towel, fastidiously cleaning her fur. Omrak was by the trapdoor, his arms held out for Daniel to pass the next piece of junk for the giant to carry away.

"I shall be back!" Omrak grunted as he lifted the broken and half-rotten chest in both hands.

"I'll be here. And ask Erin about dinner!" Daniel called. This had not been how Daniel had envisioned his first day back in Silverstone. But as he turned and surveyed the now clean abode, he could not but consider it decently spent. At least, unlike so many others, they had a place to rest.

And tomorrow, they had a Dungeon to clear!

\*\*\*

"What do you mean we aren't allowed into the Dungeon?" Daniel said, almost choking on his words.

"Your Guild identification is invalid for Silverstone," the guard at the Dungeon entrance said, his voice filled with boredom.

"But I got it updated in Karlak!" Daniel protested. "And I entered this Dungeon before!"

"You might have been brought in by a registered member, but you, yourself are not qualified. You'll need to visit the Adventurers Guild and receive your grading. This is Silverstone," the guard stressed the last word, almost as if the very name could underline the difference between their grand city and a small Beginner Dungeon town like Karlak.

Daniel sighed, finally giving up on convincing the guard to let them in. Muttering under his breath, Daniel led his friends to the Guild Hall. It seemed that being an Advanced Adventurer had significantly more rules than he had expected. On further thought, Daniel nodded his head in

31

agreement. Since the gap between Advanced and Master Classes were so high, it made sense that the Guild would want to categorise Adventurers more. It even made sense why Beginner Adventurers were generally not included in this – many Beginner Adventurers never progressed beyond that rank. Many never even progressed past the first few floors of a Beginner Dungeon as they found the danger and violence of the lifestyle too great for their constitution. Better to focus development on those that truly desired to grow.

Having been to the Silverstone Guild Hall many times before, neither Asin nor Daniel was at all shocked by the sight that greeted them. However, for Omrak who was still struggling with the grandness of the city, the lavish and magnificent Hall was a revelation. While intellectually the Northerner had known that being an Adventurer was a profitable business, it was for the first time that he understood concretely both the reach and wealth the Guild could command.

Silverstone's Guild Hall was a three-story building that took up two normal building lots with two separate, massive entrances and a gated yard for training laid out behind the hall itself.

Considering the hall was built in the middle of the city, even the unpolished Northerner understood that such use of land was expensive. The building itself was set above ground-level, with wide, bannister-less staircases leading to the two entrances. The building itself, like many others, was clad in the same white clay, insulating those within. Unlike other buildings, however, enchantment runes gleamed in regular intervals across the building, ensuring that the clay and the building itself were both protected and clean. It made the entire Guild stick out even further in this crowded city. Early in the morning as it was, Adventurers streamed out of the entrances at a rapid pace, many fully armed and armored while enterprising merchants hawked their wares and services.

"Come on," Daniel urged Omrak, breaking the blond from his trance. Omrak nodded firmly, quickly following the pair.

"Why are there two entrances?" Omrak asked. The perceptive Northerner had already noted that one entrance was less popular. Many of the Adventurers passing through those doors were both less expensively clad and less well equipped, often wearing lighter armor than the Adventurers who passed through the more popular entrance.

"Quests and Dungeons. We're headed for the Dungeon entrance," Daniel explained to his friend.

"Ah! I recall Hero Asin and Hero Daniel speaking of their outstanding deeds in Silverstone!" Omrak said, crowing.

"Yeah, outstanding," Daniel said, his face going carefully blank as he recalled one particularly memorable incident with an Alchemist. Never again would they be guinea pigs.

Inside the Guild Hall, a long snaking line lead to a familiar scene. No matter the size and location, Adventurer Guilds always seemed to look and feel the same. A single line that led to tables or counters where harried Guild Clerks awaited the Adventurers, taking loot and Mana Stones. Overseeing the Clerks were the Administrators, on-hand to deal with potential problems, assess rarer loot pieces and confirm assessments of Mana Stone prices when challenged. Hanging above, a large sign indicated the current purchase price for the most common loot items and Mana Stones.

Standing in line, the trio looked around curiously in an attempt to soak in new knowledge. There were a significant number of things to review and learn for the newcomers. The type of weapons commonly wielded both indicated the kind of dungeon environments and monsters they might meet as well as trainer specializations in the city itself.

The sword was, as always, a popular weapon, though Daniel noted a higher than normal number of individuals wielding maces and hammers. There were even a few Adventurers who carried such blunt weapons as secondaries. That likely meant either a preponderance of skeletons or heavily armored monsters. Unlike Karlak, shorter pikes, quarterstaffs and spears were carried by some groups, an indicator that tight and often cramped quarters were unlikely – at least in one dungeon. Lastly, all groups had at least one, if not more, ranged weaponry. From Asin and Daniel's experience, this was likely to deal with the flying Imps and other, long-ranged and flying monsters.

Armor too told its own story. Not a single Adventurer in sight was bereft of a type of armor, whether it be lighter and more mobile untreated leather or chainmail or bulkier and heavier defensive equipment like Daniel's plate armor. Daniel absently did note that even here, his full set of iron plate was rare, most Adventurers both preferring either lighter fare or had progressed to full steel plate. Still, the overwhelming presence of such pieces of armor showcased the greater danger these Dungeons held.

Asin, on the other hand, was the first to note the prevalence of enchanted equipment. Unlike Beginner Dungeons where most Adventurers had at most one piece of enchanted equipment, the Adventurers in this building often sported multiple pieces of equipment. The most common sight was an accessory of some sort, protective gear and an enchanted weapon. Omrak, with no such equipment, was an unusual sight, one whose presence highlighted their newness.

Team mixes were less useful as an indicator. After all, teams might have injured, sick or otherwise indisposed members who were not present at the Guild Hall. Few teams had the luxury of a Healer on hand and as such, must either soldier on through pain and injuries, use precious and expensive healing potions or make do without that member. In addition, not every team member was required for the sale of Mana Stones and loot. With most Adventurers having a keen idea of the value of the goods they had collected – and the in-built trust that guarding each others' backs engendered – the distribution of earnings later on in a more comfortable environment was common.

As such, it was of no surprise to Daniel to see what looked to be teams of two, three or seven standing in-line or outside it. Still, a few things could be gathered. The makeup of Adventurers in Silverstone was more varied than Karlak. Ranged weapons, polearms and sword wielders were common, but so were lighter clad Adventurers, many who seemed significantly less muscular than their compatriots. These were fast moving fighters like Asin or potentially spellcasters or their ilk - individuals who harnessed the power of Erlis directly. Still, like most things involving magic, they were rare. Even in the cavernous hall that was the Guild, Daniel could only easily spot maybe a dozen such individuals.

Loot that these Adventurers carried told their own story. While Mana stones continued to the majority earnings for most Adventurers in the Dungeon, loot drops could appear. Sometimes, those loot drops were of no use – Kobold Shivs from Karlak came to mind – but like the pack rats that they were, Adventurers would often bring up anything they deemed even mildly profitable. And so, before their eyes, they saw rolls of carpet, obsidian pincers, gooey eggs sacs and even a live fish deposited on the loot tables. The Clerks, used to such scenes, never even batted an eye, only on a few occasions calling for help in valuation.

The last thing the trio noticed was the preponderance of guild badges. Some were badges that Asin and Daniel had a little experience with – the wreath of red roses for the Red Roses, a simple Green Robin 'on a background of blue, the Burning Fields ornate badges – but there were more, many more. The badges were all simple, easy to note and process. A skull with a sword and mace crossed over it, a single pair of cat eyes, purple flames on a field of black, seven simple stones. There were so many that it was more of a surprise to see an Adventurer without a guild badge than the other way around.

"Next!" The Clerk's voice broke Daniel's observations. Together, the three Adventurers hurried forward to the waiting bureaucrat.

"Yes?" the Clerk said impatiently.

"We're new Advanced Adventurers. Just cleared Peel and Karlak. We need to be registered?"

"Registered and tested," the Clerk said. "Hand on the ball. One gold piece registration fee. You'll be given your testing chit once paid. Go out the backdoors to the training field and give it to Seth."

Reluctantly handing over the gold piece, Daniel watched as the crystal ball glowed, registering his new home Adventuring Guild in Silverstone.

"Who's Seth?"

"The man behind the table," the Clerk snorted, sliding the gold coin away and handing over a simple wooden board marked with a pair of scales on it. "Next!"

Daniel paused, uncertain for a moment, but he stepped aside as the Clerk shot him an impatient look. Asin quickly stepped forward, whispering the word 'Same' and proceeded to receive the same spiel. Rather than crowd the table, Daniel walked to the back door to wait for his friends.

*\*\*\**

"Newbie Adventurers eh? We can do this two ways," Seth said when the trio offered him their chits. It was obvious, now that they were here, why the Clerk felt explaining who Seth was did not require any additional words. He was the only Clerk in the back and, being a Turtlekin, extremely obvious.

"Two ways?" Omrak asked. "I seek not to receive false accolades."

"Northerner, aren't you?" Seth said with a roll of giant eyes. "No false accolades given here. We're the Silverstone Adventurers Guild. No, the first way is easy. I mark you guys as Red Advanced Adventurers, and you can start delving immediately."

"Red?" Daniel asks, Asin quietly nodding behind.

"Red is the lowest form. We use a colour system to stratify Adventurers. Goes red, orange, yellow, green, blue and white. You can advance in your colour standing in one of two ways. Either breach the necessary level in the Dungeon – the Dungeon level standards are posted in the foyer of each Dungeon respectively – or you come back here to test. Which is option two," Seth says.

"Test?" Omrak asked, tilting his head towards the training fields. Already, his eyes sparkled at the thought of testing himself.

"Test," Seth said. "That's what the gold piece is for. But to run the test properly, we got to push you, so you can get injured. Fair warning."

"That is of little concern," Omrak said, one hand over his head as he stretched out his arm muscles. "Hero Daniel is a mighty healer."

"Healer eh?" Seth said, swivelling his long neck to stare at Daniel with sudden interest. "Well, that changes matters. Depending on your Spells, we could upgrade you to Yellow rank immediately!"

Daniel groaned inwardly while Asin was much more direct as she poked Omrak with her claw and glared at him. The teenager had already been warned to not speak of Daniel's abilities. With magic users rare, and Healers, in particular, being extremely in demand, Daniel had already experienced the politicking and the ends the guilds would go to acquire a Healer. Still, the cat was out of the bag.

"I'm not exactly a Healer. I have a few healing spells but not the Class," Daniel said, correcting the misconception.

"What spells?" Seth said, some of his initial enthusiasm waning.

"Minor Healing II and Healer's Mark," Daniel reported.

"And your Level?"

"Ten."

"Really?" Seth said, slightly surprised now. "And you cleared a Basic Dungeon?"

"I did," Daniel said, pointing to his friends. Omrak, having grown bored with this conversation had wandered off to the training ground where he was loudly announcing his intention to take the Advanced Class test. A few Adventurers, training on the grounds, were giving the big Northerner angry glares at his proud boasting. Except Daniel knew that Omrak's volume had nothing to do with pride or a desire to publicly announce his actions but long years living on barren, windswept mountains. Asin had followed along with Omrak, probably as much out of curiosity as a genuine desire to test herself. "I completed Karlak with them actually. And we just cleared Peel too."

"Ah, good team then," Seth nodded. "Well, you might not have the same number of spells, and you're a bit under-Leveled, but I think, hmm... I could probably offer you an Orange designation. If you wanted more, you'd have to test."

"Orange," Daniel muttered. "Can I think about it?"

"Sure. It's your time," Seth said as he waved Daniel away. Nodding in thanks, Daniel walked over to watch his friends, not forgetting to take a drink from his canteen.

Already, the two newcomers were beginning to be put through their paces. In a fenced off, dirt sparring ground, Omrak faced a monster of a melee fighter, an individual so large, he made the blond Northerner look average sized. Hefting a long stick wrapped in steel, Omrak's opponent attempted to bludgeon the Northerner into the ground. Each strike between the pair was so violent that the attacks rang out through the courtyard, Omrak barely able to stay standing under the onslaught. Yet, no matter how fast or how hard his opponent swung, Omrak always managed to get his sword in place to block in time.

In another corner, Asin was running an obstacle course filled with strung ropes, sharp pits, swaying rope bridges and spinning rocks. All the while, Asin had to attack targets - with failure to do so resulting in an attack of opportunity launched against the Catkin by the invigilator who strode alongside the course.

"You joining us?" The speaker was an older woman in her forties, an eyepatch over one eye and clad in a tight leather tunic that showcased the intimidating number of muscles that clad her body. When she noticed that Daniel's attention was focused on her, she offered him her hand. "Angie."

"Daniel," he replied, shaking her hand.

"So, are you?"

"I'm just watching for now."

44

"Really. So, you're going to let the bureaucrat dictate how strong you are?"

Daniel smiled at the challenge in Angie's voice. "Seems like I'd be as strong as I am whether I take the test or not. The only difference might be the color of my designation."

"Har," Angie laughed, slapping her thigh in mirth. "That's a pretty mature way of looking at things. Surprising for one so young."

"I'm not that young," Daniel protested. Unfortunately, those with his own ethnic descent were uncommon in Brad, often leading to instances where he was mistaken for being younger than he was.

"Most of you kids are, to me," Angie said, chuckling. "But you are wrong about one thing. If you test, I'll guarantee that you will learn something. Might even save your life."

"Oh?" Daniel said, intrigued. "What?"

"Well, if I could tell you, what would be the point of the test?" Angie said with a smile. After a moment, Daniel finally acceded to her request.

"Good man. Come on," Angie pointed to an empty sparring ring, rolling her shoulders as she entered the ring.

"Wait. I'm fighting you?"

"There a problem?" Angie asked, the glowering threat by the one-eyed lady making Daniel suddenly gulp and shake his head. He never had a problem anyway, just surprise. As she glared at him, Daniel hurried forward quickly while pulling his hammer and shield off his back. Already, he had begun to regret his choice.

\*\*\*

"Yield!" Daniel croaked out loud, spitting around the sand that had entered his mouth. Legs splayed across his back, Angie had his weapon arm cranked up behind his back while she ground his body into the sand, her weight pushing down across the younger man's back.

"Eighteen seconds," one of the bystanders said laconically. "You did worse than the last time."

"Remember, just tap my body if you can't speak," Angie reminded Daniel as she got off him and helped him to his feet.

"Are you sure this is the test?" Daniel complained as he rotated his shoulder to remove the ache in it. Already, Daniel could feel the numerous bruises that covered his body. While the plate armor protected against impacts and strikes, it was also brutally uncomfortable to fall in with the edges digging and bruising his body on each landing. And it did nothing to protect from Angie twisting and yanking his body like a straw figure.

"It's my test," Angie said with a smile. "Again?"

Daniel stared at Angie, wondering how many more times he was going to be tossed to the ground. At the wide, sadistic smirk, Daniel could only sigh. It seemed the answer was 'a lot'. Still, Daniel bent to pick up his weapons and got into his combat stance again. If there was one thing that Daniel had, it was his stubbornness. You either grew a stubborn streak as a Miner or you left the Class. Under the earth, the weak and the hesitant broke.

***

"**Minor Healing**," Daniel whispered under his breath, using the vocal component to help focus his swimming mind. Having rolled over onto his knees, Daniel had to pause as the world rolled like the sea on a gusty day.

The slight warmth of Mana leaving his body, and the cold healing pressure of his Spell entering it a second later helped him focus. He felt something shift, a slight pop in his ears as the cloudiness in his thoughts parted. *Concussion. I have a concussion.*

"Oh shit, did I throw you too hard?" Angie said, bending down. "Crap, they're going to ream me out again…"

"I'll… I'll be fine. I'll just heal myself," Daniel croaked, still not realising he had spoken aloud. Khy'ra's voice came to him, reminding him.

"*Never use a healing spell on a brain injury if you have a choice. The possibility of making the injury permanent is extremely high. Our spells are no substitute for actual healing, even Healer's Mark speeds up the healing process too much. Better to take the time to treat the wound properly*

48

_and let it heal naturally,"_ Khy'ra said in one of their talks after a particularly long evening in the free Clinic they had run together in Karlak. The next part Daniel recalled clearly for in her voice was the slight incredulity, the awe that she had felt for his Gift. _"Your Gift though, that should be fine. From what you've told me, you can sense what is wrong and fix it directly."_

His Gift. Once again Daniel reached within, finding the spot where his Gift lived. He pulled on it, focusing on his mind, on his injury. As Khy'ra had eluded to, he 'felt' the wrongness, the bruising and injury, the incipient inflammation from being thrown so often. It took only the lightest of nudges, the smallest application of warmth to shunt the damage away, to clear his mind.

"Be nice to be a Healer. If we had a Healer, I wouldn't have…" Angie trailed off, visibly shaking her thoughts aside. "You good yet?"

"Just need a little more time," Daniel said softly, focusing again as he called forth his Mana. Healer's Mark, a heal over time spell sped up his regeneration, allowing his body to heal the numerous other injuries that had collected over the fight. Even the minor damage he hadn't cleared in his head from his Gift would be fixed by this wide area spell.

"Well, we're done. I'm impressed. Seventeen times. Most give up after the eleventh," Angie said. "Like somehow the number ten is the right number, the one that they had to beat to be considered tough."

Daniel laughed slightly as he slowly clambered to his feet. Angie had taken him on, shield and mace equipped, unarmed each of the seventeen times and each time, she had put him on his back before she gripped and controlled his attacking arm with consummate ease. She had dodged, jumped, punched and clambered over him like a particularly affectionate monkey, always one step ahead of Daniel. Through all seventeen times, Daniel had learnt only one thing – do not let her put her hands on him. For the moment she had her hands on him, the fight was over.

"What was that?" Daniel said as the pair exited the arena to allow another group to take over. As Daniel crossed by the waiting Adventurers, hands reached out to clap him on the shoulder in congratulations. Vocal encouragement was also added, though there was a tinge of gleeful amusement to it all too. One that Daniel felt was perhaps the kind that the long-suffering felt upon seeing another added to the list.

"Lopak," Angie said. "It's a fighting style I was trained in when I was little. Focuses on controlling your opponent's limbs and body to defeat them."

"But surely, it's more dangerous…" Daniel trailed off, glancing at his shield and mace that had been of little use in their fight.

"Har! Of course, it is. I'm not recommending you trade your weapons away. Just that it's worth knowing what to do when your opponent is too close for you to wield them," Angie said with a nod. "You'd be surprised how often a little knowledge like that could save you."

Now that he was no longer focused on his own suffering, Daniel noted that Omrak was currently showcasing his strength to all, going through a circuit of lifting, pulling and carrying exercises in one corner. To Daniel's experienced eyes, he realised that Omrak had not gotten off unscathed from the fight with his movements slightly more stiff than usual. In another corner,

51

Asin was sparring with Omrak's previous opponent. Though perhaps sparring was the wrong word as Asin ran around the arena, throwing her knives and otherwise harrying the Adventurer who attempted to catch her.

"Your friends are doing well," Angie said, seeing where Daniel's attention had been drawn. "You're still all Red badgers, but in a few weeks, I dare say you might qualify for Orange. If your Catkin had a few more enchanted pieces, maybe even now."

Daniel nodded at her words. Asin was, without a doubt, the fastest and most agile of the group. She seemed to have a second sense for where attacks would come from as well, a fact that frustrated Daniel and Omrak in their sparring sessions. If it wasn't for the fact that she had difficulty injuring others, Daniel would undoubtedly consider her the most dangerous of the group.

"Well, what are you waiting for?" Angie said, clapping Daniel on his back and pointing to the obstacle course. "You're not done yet."

"But…"

"No buts. No waiting around for your Mark to finish," Angie said with a sniff. "You don't always have the luxury of healing in the Dungeon."

Groaning, Daniel strode over to the obstacle course, a thread of dread already running through him. He hated obstacle courses. At least, he consoled himself, they were not as bad as puzzle rooms. Puzzle dungeons could burn with Ba'al.

\*\*\*

Hours later, the trio stared at the simple red sheath that now covered their Guild cards. The other Adventurers called it a badge, but really, it was a simple cloth sheathe that stored their cards. A physical reminder for the world that not only were the group Advanced Adventurers, but they were the lowest of the low in that group.

Yet for all that, the trio found themselves grinning as they strode back to their attic in the Lonely Candle. It might not have been much, but now, they had a goal. And the ability to enter the Dungeon the next day.

---

\*\*\*

Later that evening, Daniel found himself seated in a corner, a single candle the only illumination as he painstakingly worked on the letter before him.

*Dear Khy'ra,*

*Well, we're in Silverstone now. We finally cleared the Peel dungeon, and I've hit Level 10! Now I have the Level to go with my status of an Advanced Adventurer. The city, as mentioned, is big. Omrak wandered around, wide-eyed all of today. It was kind of funny actually, even if we did have to beat off a few pickpockets. I'm not sure he noticed.*

*We're currently staying in the Lonely Candle. The innkeeper is nice; she reminds me a lot of Elise. Do say hi to her for me as well as Litzburn and Liev.*

*Talking of Liev, how come I didn't know he was the Guild Master? Was it just me? He never put on any airs; I just thought he was a senior clerk. I don't think I'd have spoken to him the way I did if I had known.*

*In Silverstone, the Adventurers Guild has a training grounds staffed with old Adventurers. Met a very strange woman today who kept making me eat dirt for our testing.*

*I'm now officially an Orange tier Advanced Class Adventurer. They wanted to give me the Yellow tier because of my Healing spells, but I refused. It feels a bit wrong, just because I have a little knowledge. It feels unearned.*

*I know, you've cautioned me again and again about how useful healing is. How important it is. But, it just seems strange. Learning healing, even Healer's Mark from you, it never felt earned.*

*I'm sorry. You probably heard enough of this from me before. I miss you. Hope things are going well. Say hi to everyone.*

*Love,*

*Daniel*

Staring at what he had written, Daniel could not help but grimace. It sounded like he was whining. But, paper was expensive and what he had written was the truth. Khy'ra knew better anyway, to ignore his whining, his complaints. He was sure she'd read between the lines.

# Chapter 3

Morning. It was going to be a glorious morning, Omrak thought as he bounced lightly on his feet outside the Lonely Candle. As always, both Asin and Daniel were slow, taking their time to exit the building because, well, because that was them. Omrak would be frustrated if there was not so much to see!

Even early in the morning as it was, raining as it was, Silverstone was busy. In the last five minutes, Omrak was sure he had seen more people – more different people – than his entire village held. There was the baker and his assistant, working hard at producing the fresh, unleavened bread that was in demand. They even made these tasty sweet buns, ones that sold nearly as quickly as they emerged from the oven, at an outrageous price of ten copper.

Down the street, farmers and labourers arrived from the nearby village, intent on bringing their produce to market. There were so many farmers that the city had multiple markets that ran every day. Dedicated grocers purchased these goods as well from various farmers, selling the produce on to the hungry populace for a little convenience. They had so much abundance that

Omrak had even seen some grocers throwing perfectly good food – food that was just a little rotten – away last night.

"Omrak!" Daniel's voice called to him, and Omrak turned from his people watching, grinning at his friend. "Get out of the rain. Or at least put something on your head."

"Ah, Hero Daniel, this is wonderful weather. Why would you seek to hide from it?" Omrak said, shaking his head and leaning his head back to once again enjoy the downpour.

"Because you'll get sick and cold," Daniel said, shaking his head. Omrak just laughed boisterously, more so when he heard Daniel mutter about him lacking the sense to get out of the rain. Asin snorted, wrapped tight in a slick woolen cloak that shed the water. Rather than take part in the argument, the young Catkin had taken off towards their destination.

Their destination. Omrak's grin widened as he strode forwards, barely noticing how the smaller Southerners all scrambled to get out of his way. They were going to a new Dungeon today. Porthos it was. What a strange name. But Southerners were very strange. The land had been conquered, split and reconquered so many times that many names of places came from other kingdoms. But that was why Brad was so interesting.

"Remember, Omrak, we're just going to explore the first floor today. We might not even make it to the first Overseer. It's a very big floor, and while we purchased a floor crystal, with the way the walkways move, it's not as useful as you'd think."

"Of course," Omrak rumbled in agreement. Still, at the mention of the floor crystal, Omrak could not help but glance down at Daniel's waist. The map crystal was an amazing piece of enchanting, even if they were mass-produced and would require charging in a month. It had cost them nearly all their remaining gold, pooled together. But with it, the team did not have to concern themselves about getting lost in the massive first floor. After all, Daniel's extremely useful **Mapping** skill required that he actually visit said location before. And with the walkways supposedly moving, previous paths might not necessarily hold true any longer.

This time, the trio was not stopped at the gate after they flashed their newly acquired badges. They were even wished well by the guards, a blessing that Omrak returned heartily. Facing the silvery portal, Omrak bounced on his feet once again and began a series of long, slow stretches, working out the kinks and aches in his body. Rather than using friend Daniel's precious Mana, Omrak had decided to forego the healing. It was, in the end, better for his body to adapt to the strain that he placed on it gradually. Magic, while useful, was no replacement for hard work!

"Ugh!" Omrak grunted as he stepped through the portal, walking forwards immediately to join his friends at the corner of the platform they were on. The portal had sucked away some of his body heat on transit, a side effect of being sodden to the bone, and left him slightly chilled.

"Beautiful! It reminds me of home. Except for the moving walkways. And the floating platforms. And the lack of rocs and harpies," Omrak said to his friends as he drank in the view before him. As mentioned by the Northerner, the first floor of Porthos consisted of a single, expansive cavern whose bottom and top could not be seen by the naked eye. Low hanging clouds floated through the cavern, occasionally obscuring floating stone platforms, while beneath them, a never-ending mist roiled. Stone walkways, some wide enough to drive a caravan on, others barely large enough for a single person to walk, connected platforms. The never-ending groan of moving stone echoed continuously through the titanic cavern as walkways mysteriously moved, connecting new platforms without rhyme or reason.

"Right. So, nothing like home," Daniel said with a smile. Already, he had shed and stored his travelling cloak and loaded his crossbow. Omrak glanced at the long-ranged weapon and quickly put on his skullcap to cover his head as well as a metal gorget for around his neck. It was not that Daniel was a bad shot. It was that he was a terrible shot. And yet, he persisted in using that weapon.

"Very well. I shall lead," Omrak announced and pulled his sword from its sheath across his back. At first, the group were crowded together with other Adventurers exploring the floor, but as walkways split and split again, the initial crowd slowly faded, leaving the trio alone but for another party a few hundred meters behind them.

It was as the group were striding across a walkway four feet wide that the Dungeon monsters launched their first attack. A dozen Imps came screeching down from the clouds - scaled, warty figures gliding down on bat-like wings. The monsters were mostly black with shades of red that highlighted claws, pointed ears, and sharp, needle-like teeth.

"Imps!" Asin called out a second before Omrak and Daniel chimed in. Already, the Catkin had knives in her hand, assessing the arc of descent of the attackers before she threw.

Omrak had his own hatchets, but those throwing axes were precious to him. Rather than waste funds on potentially losing his weapons forever, Omrak much preferred to bat these monsters out of the air. As a trio of Imps neared him, Omrak launched himself into the air with a sudden jump, his attack catching everyone by surprise. A quick swing of his sword caught two of the three Imps leading the charge, slicing part of a wing off in one case and in another, tearing open its body. Not to be left out of the fight, the third

Imp swiped a claw across Omrak's face, foiled by a sudden duck of the neck. Even so, the attack left a light scar across his skullcap.

As Omrak landed, he snarled and shook the monster that still hung on to life off his blade, stepping forwards to quickly stomp on the struggling creature. Behind, the injured Imp managed to land, precariously, on the edge of the walkway before furling its wings and running to launch itself against Asin.

"No. You are mine!" Roaring, Omrak triggered his skill **Champion of the North.** All around, Imps that had flown past and were returning, and those already engaged with his friends, turned and charged the Northerner. Crouching low and grinding his feet into the walkway, Omrak readied himself.

Even as the nearest Imp threw itself at him, Omrak had time to focus on his friends. Daniel was dashing past Asin as he chased his own attackers. His slow and heavy tread were not quick enough, but Asin had taken the opportunity to attack the fleeing opponents' legs, hamstringing, cutting tendons and otherwise crippling the monsters. This gave Daniel time to catch up and begin his own attacks, his crossbow discarded and forgotten on the walkway.

Then, Omrak had no further opportunity to review the actions of his friends as he swung his sword in large, looping patterns. The movement itself was not expected to hit any Imps but to keep them away, to distract and anger while his friends dealt with the strays. Of course, facing nearly eight enemies at this time, Omrak could not guard all attacks, especially those that came from behind.

"Face me, you cowards!" Omrak roared as he felt another cut on his back, just below the hemline of his leather tunic. Omrak snarled as he spun around, a light red glow suffusing his body now. This was his other ability, the **Rage of Mountains**, that took over. It gave him strength, it gave him speed, and it even gave him a slight defense against attacks.

"Good work, Omrak!" Daniel called as he finished smashing down his last Imp and then rushed forwards, using his **Shield Bash** to stun another. He quickly laid into it while Asin, hopping on top of an unsuspecting Imp, launched herself into the air to stab another Imp, bearing down on its body. Her eyes widened as the creature, in a desperate attempt to get away, twisted in mid-air, taking her away from the platform by a bare foot.

"Asin!" Omrak shouted in panic. Acting purely on instinct, the Northerner thrust his sword forwards towards where she fell. Twisting, Asin dodged the thrust but grabbed the blade with her paws, her daggers falling beneath her. With a grunt and a motion that nearly caused him to fall, Omrak continued to swing his sword to bring the Catkin back onto the platform.

Rather than leave him alone, the remaining free Imps pounced on Omrak, claws unsheathed as they tore into his lightly armored legs and clambered up to tear at his arms. The red glow suffused his body further, and for the first time, Omrak triggered his new Skill.

"**The Lightning's Call**!" Omrak roared, the red around his body dissipating as it was used up in an explosion of lightning. Imps, both those on his body and nearby, were shocked, the attack striking and stunning the infernal creatures. Using the brief moment of respite, Omrak brought his sword down on one shocked Imp, splitting it in half. Asin, on her feet, stabbed another in its kidneys repeatedly as she held it tight to her while Daniel bashed another to the ground with shield and hammer. Within moments, the remaining Imps were killed, leaving the Adventurers breathing hard and bleeding.

"You're injured again," Daniel tutted, shaking his head. A moment of concentration allowed Daniel to place the **Healer's Mark** on Omrak's body before the smaller, narrow-eyed Adventurer began to treat Omrak's wounds more mundanely. Combining mundane, simple healing practices helped his spells be more effective and ensured that even if wounds weren't fully healed, they would not grow worse.

"New Skill?" Asin asked as she wandered the walkway, searching for Mana stones.

"Yes!" Omrak said with pride. "It was my pick at my last Level up. But it requires rage to use. The greater the amount of rage I have, the greater the effect."

"Useful," Daniel acknowledged as he wrapped Omrak's leg. Omrak meanwhile pressed down on a persistent wound in his upper arm, stemming the bleeding while he waited for the spell to do its work. "Now, let's talk about what happened. And what we won't be doing again. Like jumping."

Both Omrak and Asin ducked their hands in embarrassment, taking the admonishment silently before listening to Daniel's perspective of the battle. Soon, Omrak knew, it would be his turn to speak.

***

The grind as Daniel called it took hours. By common agreement, the group had planned to spend the first half of the day exploring and the second half making their way back. During that period, their main focus was to develop their combat skills and coordination against a new type of enemy. The time taken now, to learn and progress slowly, meant less pain and danger. It was a hard lesson to learn, Omrak mused. One that he had refused to learn until he was coupled with Asin and Daniel.

Perhaps it was their lack of strength. Asin was gifted and skilled, fast with her knives and highly perceptive. But she lacked strength to harm the highly armored. The overly large monsters. Whether it was Creller or Ogre, Asin reached her limit in battling such monsters quickly. Daniel on the other was strong – for a Southerner - but he lacked the ability to overpower his opponents or the courage to trade blows directly. Daniel was a rock turtle, one that hunkered beneath its protective shell, taking occasional bites at its enemy. Rock turtles were hard to kill but easy to outrun. It was just that, often, it was better to avoid them than to antagonise the rock turtle.

Still, for all their caution, all the time they spent practising fighting together, both on narrow walkways and on firm platforms, their planning had not covered this scenario.

"Are you sure that this was the way we came?" Omrak groused.

"Yes," Daniel said, staring around the empty platform. Outside of the single walkway they had used to arrive here, there were no others. A short distance away, barely twelve feet, was another platform. But the walkway to it was nowhere in sight. "That's where we came from."

"Well, do we backtrack?" Omrak asked, rubbing his chin. They had done so four times already, searching for a new path back. It was only due to luck and some good guessing that they had managed to reach their present position.

"It's twelve feet…" Daniel said slowly. In yesterday's test, the armored Adventurer had been able to achieve that distance with a running start. If Daniel removed his armor now, the distance should not be a problem. Except that the platform was not particularly large. A mistake would guarantee them falling.

"Rope," Asin hissed, already pulling out the piece of equipment from her backpack. A moment later, she had a series of metal anchors in hand, staring pointedly at the hammer in Daniel's hand.

"Hey, this is a weapon you know. Not a tool," Daniel protested, clutching his enchanted weapon. Asin's snort and outstretched hand offered her view on this.

"Come, Hero Daniel. We must all sacrifice," Omrak said, gently plucking the weapon from Daniel. Together, he and Asin quickly affixed a series of anchor points to the ground and threaded the rope through it. Asin finished tying herself off within seconds and without a word, leapt the distance. She had not even bothered with a running jump, her powerful legs bunching beneath her as she soared through the air.

"This is going to end in tears," Daniel muttered, but at Omrak's urging, he got ready. Rather than completely remove his armor, Daniel took off only his helmet, breastplate and shoulder pauldrons to allow him a little more flexibility. After that, he slipped into the leg harness that Omrak had made of the newly retrieved rope, cinching it tight around his waist.

"Do not fear, Hero Daniel; I shall be belaying you," Omrak said with a grin.

"Right. Don't fear," Daniel said. "Not as if I'm throwing myself off a perfectly serviceable location over an unknowable drop."

"No, you are not," Omrak said. "You are jumping off a platform."

Daniel sighed and backed off a few more feet before sprinting forwards. At the last second, he jumped, covering the distance easily. Too easily, as he soared past Asin and landed over three-quarters of the way on the platform, booted feet vainly attempting to take up his momentum. Omrak grinned as he watched Daniel's antics, both hands already on the rope. With a vicious yank, he pulled back on the rope, jerking Daniel to a halt a few inches from the fall.

"Owww!" Daniel cried as he fell. Clutching bruised hips, Daniel inhaled and exhaled for a few minutes. Behind, Omrak chuckled as he proceeded to unknot the rope and then bunched it together under his arm. Taking a few steps back, Omrak ran and jumped, landing on the platform safely. For a moment, the platform sagged a couple of inches, a motion that made all three Adventurers pale, before it righted itself. While trapped walkways were around, they had not heard of a trapped platform. Then again, Omrak taught cynically, any group that had experienced one probably had not survived.

"Lighter than air," Asin growled softly.

"The enchantment?" Omrak asked.

"Yes."

"Aye, that does seem like a reasonable suggestion," Omrak said, all of them peering over the edge together. Yet, a part of Omrak wondered if there really was a floor. After all, this was a Dungeon. With a shrug of his broad shoulders,

Omrak dismissed the matter. Better to die in a Dungeon, serving all, than at home, starving from a bad winter. "Come. We have much to see!"

\*\*\*

"Hero Daniel?" Omrak called, frowning as he turned to find the man standing still and a distance behind them, peering down into the mists. Omrak smiled slightly, glad that his party mates did not suffer from vertigo, unlike some others he had noticed.

"There's something down there," Daniel said softly.

"Down there?" Omrak frowned and leaned over the edge. All that met his gaze were rolling mists, cloudbanks of soft whiteness that occasionally rolled aside to showcase other, lower, platforms. But all those were a distance away. "The platforms?"

"No. Well, yes. A platform I think. Or something else," Daniel said with a frown. "It's right underneath us."

Asin squatted down, leaning over with one hand on the ground to stare. Omrak peeked too but seeing nothing, decided to keep an eye on the sky. While they were close enough to the entrance that the Imps were unlikely to attack them, you never knew. They might chance upon a recently respawned group.

"Land," Asin growled after a long silence, one that almost had Omrak bouncing due to boredom.

"So, I'm not seeing things," Daniel said with relief. He walked forwards to meet with Asin. "Figure about fifty feet?"

"Sixty-four," Asin said.

"We have about a hundred feet of rope…" Daniel started.

"Why?" Asin asked, frowning. They might be able to get down, but getting back up would be difficult. Climbing up sixty-four feet of rope vertically without any help would be exhausting.

"I thought I saw a chest," Daniel explained.

Asin visibly brightened at this, leaning over so far that it made Daniel inhale in fear for her. Omrak himself felt the pull of a chest and peered over the side but still saw nothing but mist. Floor chests randomly spawned in a Dungeon, staying available until it was found and then respawning a day later. They always held a large Mana Stone, one that was at least a grade higher than those regularly found in the monsters that roamed the floor. It was believed that Panqua had created these floor chests to attract Adventurers to each floor, to keep them roaming and thus cleansing the monsters.

"We shouldn't all go down," Daniel said slowly, rubbing his chin in thought. One issue with floor chests was that they often spawned near the Floor Champion – in this case, an Imp Overseer. The team was probably not ready to combat the Overseer themselves. But, thus far, the group had yet to see it. In a floor like this, close proximity might not mean much.

"I shall go," Omrak said decisively. Already, he was sheathing his sword and extracting the rope from his inventory. "Asin, anchors?"

"Yes," Asin said, quickly retrieving Daniel's axe and pounding the spikes into the floor. His face lined with concern, Daniel readied his crossbow, taking his turn to watch the skies. With practised ease, Omrak had a rope harness rigged for himself and attached to the rope, allowing him to slow his descent. Once he checked the rope and the anchors, Omrak proceeded to slide down the edge, one hand slowly controlling the rate of his descent while the other helped stabilise himself against the rope. It still meant that he swung significantly, winds and movement of his body pitching his body from side to side, but it was less. It reminded Omrak of days on the mountain, climbing with family as they sought to retrieve fallen sheep or hunted Mountain Cats.

"Is he laughing?" Daniel asked Asin incredulously, his words caught in a swirl of wind and carried down to Omrak. A shift in the wind made sure that Omrak did not hear Asin's reply. But yes, he was laughing. Which proper Hero would not?

Mist engulfed him all too soon, his friends disappearing as he continued to lower himself. His sight blocked, Omrak could only trust in his senses and judgement as he continually descended. In the mist, occasional screeches could be heard, muffled as were the slow groans of moving rock. Out of nowhere, a rock wall appeared, swinging feet away from the Northerner as it travelled to link up with another platform. Mouth dry, Omrak made himself swallow again. To be struck and to die from a stone walkway would not be very glorious. Though unusual, at least.

With a thump, his feet landed on the ground. Quickly, Omrak pulled his sword from his back and spun around, searching. Nothing. No enemies, no creatures. Having been turned around constantly, and without reference to the walkway above, Omrak could only choose to slowly walk in a circle as he searched for the chest. The Northerner left the rope still attached to his body, playing out behind him as he searched.

The plain wooden chest sat in a small depression, light dew covering its exterior. With a frown, Omrak realised that Asin was not here to verify its safety. Yet, his prior experience was still clear in his mind. After a long moment, Omrak extended his sword, placing its edge against the gap and prying the chest open, ready to leap back at any time. When no explosion or cloud of poison appeared, Omrak strode over to retrieve the Mana Stone. It was, unlike those provided by the Imps, of an impressive size. As an experienced Adventurer, Omrak could tell that it was of the same rarity grade as those the Imp contained but at least thrice the size.

"Yes," Omrak said with a grin. This would go a long way towards repairing their empty funds. With a gesture, he stored it in his inventory before sliding his sword away. This had gone better than he thought.

It was a thought that Omrak regretted moments later when the Imps arrived. Halfway up the rope, his muscles already tired from the torturous climb, the rope constantly swinging as the wind picked up, he had no way to defend himself.

"Careful!" Omrak growled. Daniel, shooting from above, nearly sent a crossbow bolt through Omrak rather than an Imp, his dreadful aim once again making its appearance. Worse, Daniel seemed to be unable to hit the fast-moving Imps at all. Already, Omrak bled from dozens of small cuts, the Imps tearing into his body as they flew past.

"Sorry!" Daniel cried as he placed the crossbow back on the ground in an attempt to reload it.

"Forget shooting. Pull me up!" Omrak cried.

"But-" Daniel hesitated for a second before he dismissed the thought, dropping the crossbow to the ground and grasping the rope. With a heave, he began to pull up his friend, a concentrated look appearing on his face. Beside the stocky Adventurer, Asin was flinging her throwing knives with abandon in an attempt to keep the Imps away from the duo above.

With Daniel pulling, Omrak was rising faster now. But the blond giant could not help but wonder how long his young friend could keep this up for. Strong though he might be, there was still a distance left. As another Imp tore into Omrak's shoulder, he gave up on those thoughts, removing a hand to snatch up a hatchet. With the rope knotted and twisted around, he could keep himself stationary with one hand. This freed him to swing his weapon with the other, allowing him to defend himself slightly.

"Stop. Moving," Daniel grunted, fingers white against the rope.

"I am defending myself!" Omrak grunted in return. A lucky swing tore off a wing. But it was a bad trade as an Imp plunged its claws into Omrak's

78

left bicep, tearing at the muscle. His arm bereft of strength, Omrak began to slide down, only halted as he dropped his hatchet to grab at the rope with his now free hand.

"Asin!" Daniel called urgently. The Catkin launched a vicious kick against the pair of Imps harrying her, sending them scrambling back and giving herself a second to peer over the edge. Seeing Omrak's precarious position, she tossed her knife down, activating her skill **Fan of Blades.** The suddenly multiplied projectiles fell around the Northerner, one nicking his kicking feet and another managing to impale an Imp in the back.

"Five more feet," Daniel grunted to himself. His eyes had grown slightly distant, the needs of the moment forcing him to focus. An Imp, taking Asin's distraction as an opportunity, landed behind Daniel and thrust its hand forward to no avail. The layered iron breastplate gave Daniel sufficient protection, especially against a monster that fought on instinct alone.

As the top of the walkway came into sight, Omrak threw his hand over it quickly, using the momentum to help swing his own leg above. With

Omrak's weight gone from the rope, Daniel staggered backwards and in a split-second decision, decided to go with it. His armor-clad form fell, catching the Imp behind him by surprise and crushing the smaller, winged, infernal monster beneath him.

Cheated of their easy prey, the Imps raged and threw themselves at the trio, ignoring caution and their winged advantage. For the next few minutes, the trio fought back to back, fending off razor-sharp claws and jagged teeth. In the end, the better experienced and equipped Adventurers were victorious, if not without injury.

"**Healer's Mark**," Daniel said with a groan, throwing the spell on Asin as he touched her. Forced to fight in close quarters, the lightly armored Catkin had a long cut across her chest that bled freely and another along her thigh. Both would have required stitches in another setting, but with magical healing available, Daniel pushed the wound closed before bandaging them tight. "Don't move for a few minutes. Let the spell work."

"How close are you?" Omrak asked, having finished tying off the wound around his bicep. He too had the cheaper spell cast on him already.

"I have enough for one more Minor Healing," Daniel said. Both party members understood though why he refused to use it yet. With Mana taking nearly a quarter of the day to fully regenerate, Daniel could not afford to waste the spell in case of another more serious wound. "Tell me at least that there really was a chest."

"There was. And it was not trapped!" Omrak said with good cheer. "I have the Mana Stone."

"Good. Very good." Daniel sighed and sat back down, his eyes half-closed.

Omrak, seeing the exhaustion in his friend, fell silent after moving to put his back to the group. Together, the trio sat on the walkway, watching for trouble. Still, Omrak found himself smiling. They had a floor Mana Stone and just over two score Imp stones. A very decent haul for a single day.

# Chapter 4

"You are that new team, aren't you?"

The voice broke into the trio's peaceful interlude as they sat next to the fireplace in the Lonely Candle. With autumn just beginning to make a showing for itself, the fire was not lit as the packed bodies within the inn and the lingering heat from the day was sufficient to keep the inn warm. Too warm for the Northerner. Before them was a Silverstone special, a dish called 'pizza' that both Asin and Daniel had tasted before and found to their liking. This inn seemed to have added a plethora of cheese to it though.

"I guess?" Daniel said, brows furrowed as he regarded the speaker. Standing at just over five feet tall, Daniel might have called him a dwarf if he had not met an actual member of that race before. No, this was just a shorter, very tanned individual with a neatly trimmed goatee and bad manners.

"Good. I am the vice guild master of the Seven Stones. We need a healer. We'll pay a salary to you whether you delve or not and silver for each member you heal. You'll also get double shares for any guild delve you take part in," the short man said.

"Uhh…" Daniel blinked, staring blankly at the guild master.

"Don't be taken in by this cheater," a husky, seductive voice interrupted Daniel before he could say anything further. The speaker was an older lady, probably in her mid-thirties, clad in a tight dress and an armored bodice. Daniel absently noted that her dress would really not protect much, the way it held up her bosom. Then again, perhaps it wasn't meant to, considering how nearly all the men in the room were focused on the speaker. They weren't in the Dungeon at the moment, after all. "Nicole Novak. Guild master of the Bent Nails."

"Bent Nails?" Daniel said, blinking.

"They are a women's group," the Seven Stones vice guild master said with a snap. "They don't take men."

"We don't take most men. Most are crass and annoying and blunt," Nicole said as she looked pointedly at her opponent.

"I'm not really looking to join any guilds," Daniel said, interrupting the pair.

"Don't be stupid. Everyone says that before they realise how hard it is to progress without a
84

guild. We have special deals with merchants, access to alchemists and enchanters for specialised potions, maps and journals about all these dungeons. You'll progress three times as fast as doing it alone."

"Still…"

"Leave it be, Gadi," Nicole said. "He obviously doesn't want to work with you." Turning to Daniel, Nicole leaned over the table, giving the young man an eyeful as she continued. "But do make sure to think about us. We do make exceptions for exceptional individuals. And I can tell, you are one. And I know many of my members are just looking forward to meeting you…" Asin cleared her throat, breaking the sudden silence that had fallen over the table. Straightening up, Nicole smiled at Asin and inclined her head to her. "And we can always take in your friends too."

"Oh, you shameless-" Gadi began and then stopped when the innkeeper appeared next to his elbow, the matronly woman smiling widely at him. The vice guild master then turned to her and offered a strained smile. "No offence meant."

"This is an inn. You're all welcome to be here - if you're buying," Erin said pointedly

"I got a table," Gadi said hurriedly, pointing over to his friends. "I'll just be going back there then."

Erin continued to smile widely as Gadi hurriedly retreated. When she turned to look for Nicole, she noted that the Guild Master had also taken the opportunity to disappear. Troublemakers sorted, she turned to regard Daniel. "So. You're a healer, are you?"

"Yes…" Daniel said slowly.

"Good on you. If the guilds bother you, just holler. I don't let them bring their recruiting or other beef into my inn," Erin said firmly. "And I don't want to see you bringing it in. Hear me?"

"Yes, ma'am," Daniel said hurriedly.

"Good boy. You and your friends are quiet and neat, so I'm happy to have you here," Erin said one last time before she hurried off to deal with the next impending crisis in her inn. This one involved a lack of beer at least.

"I feel inadequate," Omrak said with a chuckle. "It seems that my strength is insufficient to garner attention."

"Healer," Asin said simply, pointing to Daniel. And then, to emphasise her point she reached over and poked Omrak's left arm where the bandage covered his still-healing wound. "Useful."

"True. And that hurt," Omrak said, yanking his arm away from Asin. Without the spells, including the last one that Daniel promised to cast later tonight, it was unlikely the trio would dare to venture into the Dungeon tomorrow. It would be at least a week before they were sufficiently healed to attempt it after their last fight. Purchasing sufficient healing potions to do the same would have removed nearly all the profits from this delve.

"Split?" Asin asked.

"No. Let's do it upstairs," Daniel said after a moment's thought. While they had often split their earnings back in Karlak in the open, there, the community had been much smaller and more tight-knit. Here, they were all strangers. Better to be safe.

"Okay." Asin nodded. After a moment she fished out some coins, placing them on the table as payment. Daniel nodded as he tried to hide his yawn, exhausted as well. Healing and casting so many healing spells was tiring.

***

"I'm thinking we should go shopping first," Daniel said quietly over breakfast the next morning. Rather than eat in the overcrowded inn below, the trio had picked up their bowls of oatmeal, a platter of bacon and eggs and taken it up to their attic after voracious promises to bring the bowls down afterwards.

"Shopping?" Asin asked, tail wagging slowly.

"Well, I'd like to see what other people do to deal with the Imps. And I want to get pricing on the *Lighter than Air* enchantments," Daniel explained. "Is there anything you all need?"

"More knives," Asin said, patting her knife harness. While it was still full, Daniel knew that she had lost nearly half of those she had thrown yesterday.

"A hatchet would be good. And perhaps stronger pants," Omrak said, glancing at the leg coverings he had darned last night. "And we should identify the dagger."

"Okay then. It looks like we have a plan. Together or…?" Daniel trailed off, unsure.

"Split," Asin answered immediately.

"I would welcome company," Omrak said at the same time. Daniel glanced at the youngster who, uncharacteristically, looked slightly nervous. After a moment Daniel realised that Omrak probably was nervous – this was a very large city. Especially for someone who had spent most of his life in a tiny village in the mountains.

"Then Asin will go on her way, and Omrak and I will go shopping," Daniel said, smiling. "We'll take today off. Maybe get some training in this afternoon."

Asin offered a quick nod, licking up the last of her oatmeal before she scrambled out of the attic. Daniel frowned slightly, curious about why the Catkin was so eager to go off on her own but after a moment decided against it. Friend or not, she had a right to her privacy.

"Come, let us journey henceforth!" Omrak said as he chewed on the remainder of the bacon. "I look forward to the exploration of this great city."

"Yeah. That too," Daniel said, rubbing his chin. "Let's make sure to ask Erin about where to go first though."

"As you wish, Hero Daniel."

\*\*\*

"Enchanters? Hmmm…" Erin hummed, tapping the wooden spoon against the side of her face. "Well, I got a few enchantments done for the kitchen, but they're not really who you want. You're looking for the *Lighter than Air* or *Flying* ones, right? Doing Porthos?"

"Yes, ma'am."

"Well, depends on how much you want to spend. If you want cheap and serviceable, Millicent's on Magic Road is the way to go. If you want something that'll last more than a few months though, you'll want to speak with Poe down at Barbary street."

"About the expense…"

"How much would this cost, honoured innkeeper?" Omrak rumbled over Daniel.

"Har. Honored innkeeper," Erin said with a grin. "Millicent has pre-made boots with the enchantment on it starting at about twenty gold coins each from what I was told. Poe custom makes everything, so you'll be waiting a bit. It's at least fifty gold with him."

Daniel coughed, subconsciously feeling at his pouch. Not that he actually kept that much in it these days, what with his Inventory ability. That Skill made pick-pocketing Adventurers much less enticing, which, of course, was why most Adventurers stored their wealth there. Even after all their hard work and their successful run last night, he only had six gold left to his name.

"That is too expensive. I fear I shall have to brave the first floor without such aid," Omrak announced unashamedly. "Perhaps we should visit the armorer first, Hero Daniel."

"I'd still like to see them," Daniel countered and then turned back to Erin. "Thank you for your recommendations."

"Not a problem," Erin said with a wave of her hand. She hurried off back into her kitchen to check on her pot of stew while the two Adventurers left the inn, still arguing about which place to visit first.

***

The blacksmithing quarter was quite a hike away, located in the south eastern most part of the city where prevailing winds would take the constant smoke out over the Arq river or down south. It kept the majority of the city clear of the never-ending smoke from the forges and, subsequently, most people happy. The only exception being the coal merchants who had to drive around the city itself to get to their biggest customers. Luckily, the city council of Silverstone had long ago built an external semi-circular road that ran outside the city, large enough to allow wagons to pass each other abreast. Still, people being people, the merchants still complained.

Rather than spend half the day walking to the blacksmithing quarter, the pair chose to ride on one of the many public carriages that ran down the main roads. While expensive at a copper a ride, the large armored corraks moved quickly and seemed to never tire in their endless circuits around town. Of course, the carriages never stopped, so passengers had to jump on and off the transport.

Even so, in a short hour, the pair found themselves walking down the streets of the quarter, peering at working blacksmiths as they filled orders.

"Out of here, Adventures. Your street is down that way," a grumpy merchant said as she shoved her way past the two slow-moving Adventurers. Suitably chastened, the pair hurried over to the next street where, as promised, blacksmiths and armorers worked on weapons and armor.

The pair walked the streets with interest, both of them highly interested in what was being created in front of them. To Daniel's surprise, Omrak showed a surprising level of knowledge about blacksmithing, often commenting on the methods used.

"My Dad always sent me to visit Uncle Graz whenever he and my brothers were out hunting. So, I worked the bellows and occasionally made some nails," Omrak explained. "I'm no expert, and most of my work was barely acceptable for my heart was never in the steel."

Daniel nodded, understanding Omrak's point. More than that, he knew that Omrak desired to return one day to his village and purchase the land next to the family farm and settle down as a farmer.

"So, what are you looking for?" Daniel said, glancing at Omrak's pants.

"Mmm… chainmail or scale mail. Probably chain sewed into leather would be best," Omrak answered Daniel, running a hand along his legs. "I dislike the restriction of full plate. It is too hot."

"Tell me about it," Daniel muttered. Since the pair were not going to the Dungeon today, Daniel was wearing his old leather breastplate. Even then, he had to occasionally swipe at his forehead and drink from his canteen to hydrate himself. Together the pair continued to amble down the street, commenting on various weapons and armor.

"I fear we might not find what we look for here," Omrak said after a while. The pair had made their way halfway down the street already and had yet to see any pair of pants that suited what Omrak desired. The closest they had seen was a skirt-like object made of banded metal that would cover most of Omrak's thighs but still left his calves open to attacks.

"Maybe we should ask?" Daniel said hesitatingly. It was quite obvious that the blacksmiths and apprentices were extremely busy and disliked to be bothered. Still, the pair gathered their courage and stopped by to ask one particular apprentice who was cooling off.

"Armored pants?" the apprentice sniffed, shaking his head. "We don't sew here. Got good solid steel cuisse, greaves and poleyn's here, but we sell off some of our chainmail parts to the hacks up near the north. You'll find them next to the-" the apprentice hawked and spat, "-leather workers."

"Thank you," Daniel said. With their main needs sorted, the pair turned and headed back up north, though not before Omrak purchased a replacement for his hatchet. He even splurged and picked up another as an additional backup to store away.

"I see more Beastkin here," Omrak said as the pair made their way farther north as instructed. As they neared the area farther away from the river and closer to the tailors, there certainly were more Beastkin working the forges.

"No surprise," Daniel said with a sigh. While it was unlikely to be a case of overt speciesism, Daniel knew from his talks with Khy'ra and Asin that it was easy to 'lose' rental applications or to choose to rent towards other, less bestial, species. The wars with the Beastkin and their rumored ties to Ba'al continued to impact human and Beastkin interactions, even hundreds of years later. When Omrak made signs of interest, Daniel lowered his voice and explained how the world worked – as explained to him by those older and more experienced.

"I do not like such dealings," Omrak said eventually and determinedly. "One should be judged by the strength of one's arms, the honor of one's words and the depths of their courage. All else should pale."

"No, neither do I," Daniel agreed. "It's why I'm a bit hesitant about the guilds. Some of them, they don't take Beastkin. Others treat them as second-class Adventurers."

"We should not join such places," Omrak said firmly before suddenly grinning. Omrak then rushed away like a child having spotted free candy, leaving Daniel shaking his head behind him.

Sometimes, Daniel envied Omrak's ability to see things so simply. But at least in this he completely agreed with the Northerner. He would not abandon his friend for measly material benefits.

What Daniel did not mention to Omrak but which preyed upon his mind was his Gift. If the guilds were competing over him now, with his measly healing ability, their reaction when they learnt of his Gift was likely to be greater. It would be best to only join a guild that he could truly trust. One that would value and understand Daniel's own reluctance to exploit his Gift too greatly. Or else the consequences might be unimaginable.

"Come, friend, Daniel. Do these pants fit me?" Omrak roared, his loud voice cutting through even the clang of metal and the hiss of boiling water. Face flushing, Daniel hurried over before Omrak said something else embarrassing for the entire city to hear.

***

"Are you Millicent?" Daniel asked, hours later when the pair had finally left the smith quarters with one pair of well-fitting scale mail pants and one less shred of dignity.

"Depends on who's asking. If it's the tall drink of muscle behind you, I certainly can be," the old woman says, hungrily eyeing Omrak. Omrak flushed at the attention, stepping back protectively as he crossed his arms over his chest. That just made Millicent grin wider.

"We were hoping to look at some boots with the *Lighter than Air* enchantment," Daniel said as he stepped in front of Millicent.

"Yes, yes. You're new Adventurers doing Porthos. Probably not even enough gold among all of you to buy a single pair," Millicent said with a sniff and waved her hand to one corner of the shop. "The new shoes are there, but if you turn right around, you'll see some of the used ones I buy back and resell. Enchantments will be powered up before you leave, of course."

"Used?" Daniel's voice actually grew slightly excited at that. He might be able to afford those.

98

With a nod and smile, Daniel and Omrak turned to browse the boots which were nicely arrayed according to size. Unfortunately, that seemed to be the only organisation done with styles ranging from simple ankle-length boots to thigh-high pieces that had heels on them. With their disparate sizes, the pair quickly split up to browse for potential options.

Daniel was finding things much easier with six different options to choose from. While all were serviceable, some were more worn than others, and all at least required seven gold coins. The most expensive pair was nearly as expensive as a new pair at nineteen coins.

Omrak on the other hand, under the constant, smiling scrutiny of Millicent had found only one pair in his purported size. But a simple test showed that the wearer had much slimmer calves, forcing Omrak to browse the remainder of the store. The blond giant soon realised that the majority of the store catered to that single enchantment with cloaks, boots and pendants all hosting that same spell. There were, surprisingly, few cloaks available while the pendants sold were all new.

"Your variety of cloaks are low," Omrak said bluntly as he fingered one particular woolen piece.

"Not much demand. Cloaks get damaged easily during fighting," Millicent said, shaking her head. "I put the enchantments near the collar, but still, few experienced Adventurers want enchanted cloaks. Pendants now, those you can wear forever."

"Forever?" Omrak said, frowning. "I have heard spoken of conflicts between enchantments."

Millicent sniffs slightly at those words. "Oh sure, if you want to carry a dozen or more, you'll need to be careful with how they affect your aura and yourself. Especially if you're a Mana user. Big man like you, I bet you swing that sword only, right?" At Omrak's nod, she smiled. "You probably could get away with eight or nine before it's a problem. Your friend over there, the Healer? He's got to be more careful."

"I do not understand why," Omrak said.

"Don't worry your pretty little head," Millicent said. "If you're interested in those pendants, I can always work out a deal with you. Have you help around the hou... shop till you are paid off."

"Do you not fear me disappearing on you?" Omrak said, frowning.

"I'd get your Adventurers Card first, my dear," Millicent said with a cackle. "I'm not that old yet."

"I was more concerned about my potential death," Omrak corrected her. "I would never take what is not mine."

Millicent's grin just grew wider at Omrak's words. As she started to lean over to point out other pendants for Omrak to look at, Daniel stepped up quickly to Omrak's side and yanked on his elbow. When the blond giant looked at him, Daniel beckoned him down to whisper in his ear. A moment later, Omrak's face turned beet red before he turned around and left the shop, stomping out.

"Did you have to spoil my fun?" Millicent said, glaring at Daniel. One hand came up from under her counter holding a wand which she casually fingered.

"I did. I truly did," Daniel said, stepping away. "Well, I can't afford anything yet. I'll be back another time."

"No, you won't. But your friend is welcome," Millicent said bitingly.

"Yes, ma'am. I'll let him know," Daniel said as he scurried out. Outside, he looked up and down the street before he finally found his blond friend. When he caught up, Omrak was looking straight ahead, refusing to meet Daniel's eyes. *Well, this was a less than stellar shopping trip*, Daniel thought. Still, if they were here on Magic road they should be able to find someone to identify the dagger.

With that thought in mind, the pair started walking along the road, asking questions of those shopkeepers within. Quickly enough, the pair realised that the vast majority of shopkeepers were just that – shopkeepers. Very few had enchanters within, and the few that did refused to speak with them without an appointment. They were nearing the end of the road, and they had just entered a rundown, sparse shop in desperate hopes of finding someone when they encountered the gnome.

Sat on a high-chair, poring over a single bracer and gently tweaking the gold wire it was laying down, the gnome was entirely engrossed in its work. Pink hair, cut short and a workman's leather apron along with large, bulky gloves and a pair of goggles covered the enchanter's face. The pair quietly and respectfully stood aside, waiting for her to be done.

With a slight exhalation of breath, the gnome placed the forceps down, leaning back and stretching. As she did, she saw the pair and jerked backwards, uttering a low yelp as she over-balanced and fell off the chair. The pair of adventurers raced forwards, Omrak and Daniel apologising profusely while the gnome popped right back up.

"Sorry, sorry, sorry! Didn't see you customers! What can I do for you? Sara Vorfix at your service!" Sara said excitedly. "We don't have much stock right now, but if you need any commission work, I can give you the best prices in town!"

"We require an identification," Omrak said, pulling out the enchanted knife they had acquired in Peel and laying it on the counter.

"Oh." Deflated, Sara stopped bouncing as much in excitement. Still, she grabbed the knife and pulled it from the sheath, pulling a magnifying lens from her belt and beginning the examination.

In twenty minutes she finally nodded, almost to herself. "That was boring."

"Pardon?"

"It's a boring enchantment. *Snake's Curse*," Sara said. "Poison. It's a slow build poison, so it increases with each strike."

"Ah," Daniel nodded and then glanced at Omrak. The pair of them sighed, knowing that it wasn't a particularly useful enchantment. At least for them. "Do you buy enchanted weapons?"

"I do," Sara began enthusiastically and then deflated suddenly, "But I don't have the money for it right now."

"Oh."

"I could take it on commission?" Sara said slowly, her eyes wide and hopeful. "Give you a better deal."

"That…" Daniel and Omrak shared glances, noting how disreputable the store looked. Yet, Daniel had a good feeling about the gnome. "Well, maybe. What would the terms be?"

Grinning, Sara leaned forward and began the negotiations. A short while later, the pair walked out of the store, less one enchanted dagger and with the addition of a new contract. Inside, Sara was already busy cleaning the store and getting ready to display the new weapon, obviously more spirited than ever. Their business complete in the magic sector, the pair decided to move on to the training grounds.

\*\*\*

"Welcome back, boys!" Seth greeted the pair as the two strode in. "Here to use the grounds?"

"Yes, sir," Daniel said. "We're hoping to perhaps speak with one of the trainers and work with them for tactics on the first-"

"Floor of Porthos," Seth finished for Daniel, smiling. "Of course, you are. That'll be two silver."

Once the pair had shelled over the coin, they were directed to Quinn, an older man who sat squinting over a book. Surrounding the man were a wide variety of boxes and specimen jars, many containing recognisable loot pieces.

"Yes?" Quinn said.

"We were told you could help us with the Imps?" Daniel said, unsure what this man could do.

"Right, right. Imps. It's always Imps," muttered Quinn. With a snap, he shut the book and slid it under the table before turning to the chest on his right. Within seconds, he had extracted a surprisingly complete Imp specimen whose body glowed ever so slightly.

"Here we have a common Infernal Imp. As you can see, this particular specimen is considered average for its kind standing at three feet two inches tall. Now, Infernal Imps are known for attacks conducted by their sharp claws and have been known to bite prey that have angered them. In the wild, Infernal Imps are known to carry diseases and other infectious substances under their nails, but those in the Dungeon, having no such source, are 'clean.' However, Adventurers should always watch out for their flying attacks with the Imps tendency to go for crippling maneuvers. Now, as you can see here, the Imps wings are similar to the Dark Wing Bat with webbing between thin limbs. Unlike the Dark Wing Bat, there are no digits at the end of the wing…"

A half-hour later, the pair of Adventurers walked away from Quinn with a dazed look on their face, right into the arms of the smiling Armsmaster who guided them over to his corner of the training grounds. There, a series of weapons were laid out, ready to be borrowed or tested for training purposes.

"Have a good talk with Quinn?" the Armsmaster said teasingly. "Don't worry; you can always get him to explain anything you didn't understand."

"I... thank you," Daniel mumbled, staring at the weapons.

"Mateo," the Armsmaster supplied at Daniel's hesitation. "And you're welcome. Now, let's talk tactics and arms now that you have some knowledge of the Imps."

"Uhh..."

"Well, what do you know of them?" Mateo said impatiently.

"They fly. Light bones to give them flight. Low body fat, high metabolism," Daniel repeated. Unlike Omrak, with his own knowledge of biology gained through studying healing, he had understood a significant amount of what Quinn had spoken of. No longer under the onslaught of

---

information, he began to truly think. "They tire fast."

"True," Omrak said, recalling past battles. "They land after a few passes."

"And they're easy to injure because of the bones. Their skin is pulled tight, especially along the wings. Not much elasticity at all," Daniel said.

"Well, well. You were listening," Mateo said with a smile. "That's true too. Too many Adventurers fight them like they would a Harpy, but that's just a waste of good arrows." Mateo reached out to the table, hefting a strange looking crossbow. Rather than a single, narrow shaft for a bolt to sit, a hollow cylinder sat in place. A long cut ran along the cylinder, allowing the bow to be armed by sliding the end of the bowstring back which seemed connected to something within the cylinder itself. "This here is a rockbow. You use these," a hand pointed to a series of similar-sized rocks which had silver-green veins running through them, "in them. Load it in, aim and fire. Just make sure to keep it pointed up a bit, the rocks can roll out if you're not careful."

"Boom rocks," Daniel said, identifying the rocks immediately. That wasn't its official name of course, but for the Miners, it was best known by its colloquial name.

"You know of them," Mateo said slightly surprised.

"I used to be a Miner." Daniel frowned, recalling his experience with these rocks. They were an uncommon feature in the mountains but had a tendency to explode when struck too hard. The rocks themselves were solid; it was the vein of silver-grey metal that caused problems. When faced with a vein of suck rocks, Miners had to either work slowly around the vein, abandon the seam or wait for a more experienced Miner to arrive.

"Well, that explains it. The shards aren't big, and the rockbow is useless against most other monsters, but the Imps in flight get knocked out and down easily. Pepper them with these and their wings shred, forcing them to land," Mateo said. "Of course, the other option is the tank and spank."

"Tank and spank?" Daniel said with a frown. In answer, Mateo pointed to the large tower shields.

109

"Tank the attacks, wait for the Imps to get tired. And then spank them like the naughty little boys that they are."

"Ah…" Omrak walked over to the tower shields, hefting them. "I dislike such implements. But if the Imps do not face me directly, perhaps this is an acceptable response."

"That's the spirit! We rent all of this equipment out too. You'll need to leave a deposit of course, just in case you die, but it's cheaper than purchasing them outright. You'll find they're not as needed on the next floor," Mateo said, all business now.

"Thank you. I think we will," Daniel said as he hefted the rockbow.

"I'm glad you youngsters are taking this seriously. Most others, they don't understand what makes a great Adventurer."

"Courage!" Omrak said enthusiastically.

"Preparation," Daniel said softer, recalling one of the first conversations he ever had.

"That's right. Preparation. Courage can be bought. Preparation is key!" Mateo said, clapping Daniel on the hand. "I see great things in your future, young man. If you survive."

# Chapter 5

"You think he saw us?" Daniel asked as they eyed the Imp Overseer in the distance. The Overseer was on a particularly large platform, protected by a horde of Imps. The entire group seemed to be lazing around, occasionally breaking out into fights while waiting for an unlucky Adventuring group. Looking down at the group from a higher platform, the trio was slowly backing away as they debated their options. It had only been a week since their first visit to the first floor of Porthos, and while the party had managed to gain some confidence at battling the Imps, caution said they should not attempt the Overseer yet.

"Yes," Asin said, pointing. The brewing scene of chaos, where the Overseer was kicking and whipping Imps into action left a feeling of dread in Daniel's stomach. Sniffing the air, Asin turned to look around before adding. "Smell only them."

"It seems we must do battle," Omrak said, moving forwards to where the walkway connected to the platform they were on. He propped the tower shield on the ground, letting it rest for the moment while he waited.

"Ba'al's tears," Daniel swore, cranking back on the hand-held rockbow. This was his second as he'd come to realise that the heavier bows were of less use to him. In fact, Daniel had fallen in love with the weapon – his miserable aim was significantly compensated by the explosive nature of the projectile. He didn't have to hit the Imps, just get the shot near them to do damage.

Unlike the pair, Asin had not changed her weapons or fighting style. What she did sport was a new enchanted harness, one that constantly replaced the knives that she drew from it with those in her Inventory. It was a powerful enchantment, one that she had only started wearing today. Daniel was slightly surprised to see it, knowing how expensive such an enchantment could be – and the fact that Asin herself had just bought one from Tevfik not so long ago. Then again, it was not his place to dictate how she spent her money. In either case, with less concern about running out of knives in the middle of battle, Asin's effectiveness at dealing with the Imps had grown.

"Coming," Asin said, drawing Daniel's attention back. The herd of Imps had split once in the air, coming at the group from three directions. The first flew just in front of the Overseer who took its time walking towards the trio. The second and third each attempted to flank the group.

Without speaking, all three Adventurers took a corner of a triangle, leaving enough space for each of them to step back if needed while they waited. It would not be long before the first Imps, those coming directly ahead arrived. Omrak roared the **Challenge of the North**, drawing their attention to him and forcing them to attack his raised tower shield. Hunkered down low beneath the angled protection, the Imps could only crash, jump or swerve away depending on their own nature. One particularly brave Imp landed on the shield itself, hooking its claws in an attempt to pull the protection down. It was an action that would see the end of its life as Omrak would take a swift step forwards, smashing the shield and Imp into another, sending both Imps falling into the mists.

Soon after, the other wings of the attack arrived. Daniel shot and loaded as quickly as he could, pulling rocks from the carefully designed bandolier across his chest as he fought. It was, to Daniel's estimation, the safest place to keep explosive rocks – right in front of the biggest, toughest piece of armor that he had. Better than around his waist for sure. Rocks flew from the crossbow, some exploding a few feet away from Daniel and peppering him with their shards, the smaller rocks sounding like heavy rain on a metal roof as they shattered on his armor. Most of the rocks blew up a few dozen feet away from him to harass and injure the flying red monsters.

Over on Asin's side, the Catkin was focused, her hands flicking out semi-regularly as she worked more precisely. Each attack either struck an Imp or a couple as she triggered her **Fan of Knives** ability. Attacks often targeted Imps slightly ahead and above the rest, their sudden cessation of movement or torn wings creating further havoc in the sky. Unlike Daniel's scattershot approach or Omrak's stonewall, her Imps fell and stayed down.

"Overseer!" Omrak called out. The blond giant focused, pulling the large shield back into his Inventory, his face showing the strain from using his Mana in such a hurried fashion. Still, freed of the cumbersome protection, Omrak took the opportunity to charge his opponent.

"Damn it, Omrak!" Daniel snarled as their friend created a hole in their defense. At least he had waited until the initial group had left, leaving the pair a chance to recover. Dropping another rock into place, Daniel yanked the string back while searching for a good spot to aim. Finding it a moment later, he raised the weapon and triggered it, arms already aching from the constant motion. To save time, Daniel had kept his shield on his left hand, forcing him to carry the extra weight as he loaded his crossbow.

"Go!" Asin snapped as she stepped sideways to adjust her position. With a flick of her hands, she had two knives in it, held ready and low as she crouched down, eyeing the Imps which had gathered back together into a swarm.

Daniel snarled but heeded her advice, trusting in Asin to handle matters as he dropped the now empty rockbow. Reaching for his belt, Daniel pulled his hammer free as he watched Omrak take a cut across his back, the Overseer's whip leaving a burning mark on the Northerner's body where it was still unarmored. As he crossed over to aid his friend, Daniel took the time to cast a **Healer's Mark** on him as he reached his party mate.

"Side by side," Daniel said as he arrived, taking the whip high on his shield as Omrak panted. "I'll go first; you come in a step behind."

"I can do this."

Not giving Omrak time to argue, Daniel surged forwards, shield held high. Omrak snarled, following a step behind, waiting for his opportunity. The Overseer's whip swirled faster in retaliation, striking again and again at Daniel. But Daniel's plate armor and shield absorbed the majority of the attacks, the ones that slipped between the gaps left only stinging and burning cuts. Sheltered by his friend, Omrak closed the last feet in a surge of energy, bypassing Daniel as the Overseer attempted to retreat to make full use of its weapon.

Left behind by the quick retreating Overseer - and Omrak who stuck close to it, swinging his sword and fouling the creature's attempts to get away - Daniel sagged to a knee, panting from the exertion. It was only for a moment before the sound of a scuffle behind him drew his attention back to his Catkin friend. Asin grappled and fought with the last half-dozen Imps who clawed at her body, ignoring the shocks of electricity and her pendant's deflection in equal measure.

"Asin!" Daniel said, concern in his eyes as he rushed forwards. Thankfully, the way back was significantly faster without the danger of losing an eye. As he closed, Daniel triggered **Shield Bash** as he smashed his way into the pile of bodies that was holding his friend down. His move sent a few bodies flying, their lighter bodies unable to stand the mass of the stocky, armored Adventurer. A howl of pain indicated that they might not be the only ones.

**Double Strike** was triggered next, the move allowing Daniel to quickly sweep another pair of Imps aside. A particularly large Imp, perched on Asin's left hand twisted to snarl at Daniel, its teeth red with blood. This one Daniel graced with **Perin's Blow**, his gift **Find Weakness** guiding his body to target the sides of its ribs where its lungs lived. The attack blew the monster off the angry Catkin, taking another Imp with it. In a moment, Asin had rolled up while yowling in pain.

"Off!" Asin growled, pointing to Daniel's feet.

"Wha... Sorry!" Daniel said, quickly shuffling his feet aside as he got off her tail. Immediately, it twisted to wrap near her body, only the end which was stepped on not curling properly. But Daniel had no time to focus on that as the last couple of Imps recovered from their shock. The pair fell on the remaining Imps with vengeance, hammer and knives flashing as they took lives before it was finally over.

Omrak and the Overseer were still battling one another in the distance, the overly large, muscular Imp with its tiny wing nubs having discarded its whip for its claws to grapple the Northerner. In turn, Omrak had dropped his own weapon, leaving the two rolling around on the sandy floor.

"You think we should help?" Daniel asked Asin even as the pair walked over, their breathing harsh as they attempted to steady it. Asin was limping, one eye glued shut beneath a wash of blood where a strike had torn off part her forehead. A hasty bandage kept the skin in place while Daniel's **Healer's Mark** worked on her. Already, his other **Minor Healing** spell had helped to reduce her pain and injuries.

118

"Dangerous," Asin said, obviously not inclined to Daniel's sense of humor at the moment. Testing his ankle which he had somehow managed to twist, Daniel started jogging forwards, watching the pair. Already, he could feel his skill acting, guiding his thoughts. Once he was close enough, Daniel jumped, yelling out loud just before he landed next to the pair, the hammer arcing downwards already.

As Daniel's hammer connected with the back of the Overseer's head, a white flash spread across the Overseer. It wrapped the creature in the light, dancing for a moment before being absorbed back into the hammer. Next to its normal runes, a new one appeared, stylised to look like an Imp.

The attack, powered by Daniel's jump and his ability, had struck the Overseer dead-on as Omrak held the monster tight. Already injured from repeated punches and a few cuts, the Overseer gave up the last of its life, fading into motes of blue as Omrak collapsed, his hands splayed beside him. All across the uncovered portions of his body, scratches both light and deep bled.

"**Healer's Mark**," Daniel whispered, once again using the vocal component to heal Omrak. After which he forced himself to stand, Asin having scrambled close to snatch the Mana Stone and then away again, suddenly having significantly more energy as she went to pick up the remaining stones.

"Why'd you leave?" Daniel said once he caught his breath. Knowing that Asin enjoyed this aspect of the delving, Daniel was grateful for the chance to sit and rest and verify his own injuries. It was best that he do so immediately, before the adrenaline wore off and he realised he'd been bleeding for ages without realising it.

"The Overseer's weapon was too long. I could not protect you both if I had stayed," Omrak said, gesturing to where the weapon, surprisingly, had not disappeared. Asin continued to chase around the walkways, picking up the stones.

"That's pretty smart," Daniel said. In the heat of battle, Daniel had not realised that factor.

"Neither did I," Omrak said suddenly with a grin. "It was only after you joined me that I realised why I felt it right."

Daniel sighed, resting his head on the cold metal of his armor. *Damn it, Omrak. I was just beginning to respect your decision.*

"What was that with your hammer?" Omrak asked, changing the subject.

"Oh! The enchantment finally triggered," Daniel said happily. He lifted his hand, sharing the information weapon information with his friend.

### Steel Spiked Hammer

*Damage: 8 - 12 + .5 Strength + 2 Quality Bonus*

*Durability: 47/50*

*Item Class: Enchanted*

*Quality: Good (+2 bonus to damage)*

*Enchantment: Aide from Above (1/1 Summoning Stored). Hammer has 0.1% chance to store a copy of an attacked monster in it. Each stored summoning may only be used once. Summoning lasts for 5 minutes.*

"Ah! I had wondered," Omrak agreed. Asin, having wandered back, stored the whip and then sat down next to the pair, chewing on some hard tack.

"Sorry. I should probably have told you, but till now, nothing stored. My luck must have sucked," Daniel said with a sigh. "I could have sworn I've swung this over a few hundred times."

"Luck bad." Asin nodded with agreement. "No like luck enchantments. Persistent."

"But the effects are so much greater!" Omrak said, pointing to the hammer. "We now have an Overseer to use."

"Once," Asin countered.

Watching the pair begin arguing, Daniel chuckled to himself and pulled out some water and his own lunch, his body beginning to shake slightly as the adrenaline left it. Well, they had finished their first Overseer. Even if they had yet to get to the next floor.

\*\*\*

"First floor Champion Mana Stone. Eight gold two silver," the Clerk announced after a quick glance, pushing it aside and then touched the whip. "Overseer whip. Uncommon drop. We can give you seven silver for it."

"Seven?" Asin yowled, scandalized.

"It's not enchanted. Most people buy it for the novelty value locally. We ship some down south – there's a market for whips there," the Clerk replied immediately, unfazed by Asin's protest. "You can keep it and attempt to sell it somewhere else. We don't negotiate."

"Sell," Asin said distastefully. The Clerk didn't even show a flicker of surprise as she pulled the whip aside, moving on to the small pile of Imp claws and Mana stones. Soon enough, she had totaled and handed over the team's earnings.

"Pleasure doing business with you, Adventurer. We'll see you next delve," the Clerk said by rote as Asin stomped back to the waiting pair. Asin's ears twitched, tail lashing out behind her while she considered going back and giving that woman a piece of her mind. Then, considering how much that'd hurt her throat, Asin decided against it. Anyway, the Guild wasn't about to change just because one particular Catkin felt they were taking too large a profit margin. After all, Asin knew that that same Mana Stone would be sold after refinement for at least four times the price. But since it was royally decreed that Mana Stones from a Dungeon could only be sold at the Guild, there was nothing she could do about it.

"How'd we do?" Daniel asked.

Rather than speak, Asin offered the tally note to Daniel. A quick glance was all that Daniel needed but Omrak, taking the note after him struggled to read it. The past few months had the pair teaching Omrak how to read, though it was slow going as the Northerner attempted to memorise the most common symbols. For some reason, the big Northerner struggled more than he should. At least in Asin's perspective.

Such a strange thing – that these humans would allow others of their kind to be illiterate. The Beastkin might have many flaws, but all Beastkin were taught to read. Beast-script if not Brad, but more often than not, both. Without their written language, communication could easily break down between Beastkin species after all. So many Beastkin had their own clan languages that without a common script and common language, it was a recipe for failure.

"Not bad," Daniel said. "Back to the inn?"

"Busy," Asin said, shaking her head. In their own corner by the guild hall, Asin was happy to break apart the coins by feel from the pouch and hand them their share.

"Oh, okay," Daniel said. While his face showed no trace of his disappointment, the sudden shift in his scent might as well have shouted it to the Catkin. A part of Asin wondered if Daniel realised how clear his emotional changes were to her. Still, she did not explain but waved goodbye to the pair.

Omrak and Daniel needed more time together anyway, Asin thought. Since both of them were direct fighters, there was significant overlap in their roles in the team. Thus far, things had gone relatively well, but she could sense the brewing conflict. It had lessened since the pair had started spending more time together, alone, in the city, and it was something that Asin felt should be encouraged.

It also helped that she had her own things to do.

An hour later, Asin found herself in the south-west corner of the city near the walls. This portion of the city was more rundown, drier than most, which required its residents to make regular treks outside and to the north of the city to gather fresh, clean water. As such, it was no surprise that water barrels lined the streets, collecting what little rain fell. But, unlike most other quarters, the Beastkin quarters were clean of refuse and trash on the streets, the entire area filled instead with the smell of spices being cooked and dried.

"Asin," Tevfik called out to the Catkin girl a moment before he slipped his hand around her waist. She spun around, growling at him as she struggled, futilely to escape from his grasp. He chuckled, trapping her easily before he lay a kiss on her lips and nuzzled her with his whiskers. "Good day?"

"*Very good. I caught scent of the Overseer and guided the team to him. Made good gold today,*" Asin said with a purr, rumbling away happily in Catkin. The language was a lot lower, a lot more growly and involved significantly more body language which made it perfect for the bestial Catkin girl.

"*I'm surprised Daniel agreed to fight him,*" Tevfik said, eyes drawn tight. "*I had thought he was more careful than that.*"

126

"*I need to pay Mulla,*" Asin said, evading the question. Of course, Daniel was more cautious. Perhaps because he was their Healer, Daniel was always cautious. That's why she hadn't told him but guided him to her choice.

Sensing her evasion, Tevfik sighed but did not pursue the matter, instead following along as the girl scampered off to see the Apekin enchanter. "*You know that Mulla is willing to wait, right?*"

"*Because you guaranteed it. And I can pay now,*" Asin said firmly, bursting into the Monkeykin's home workshop. Soon enough, the Catkin was back out, low curses in Brad following her.

"*What happened this time?*"

"*Walked in on him cleaning,*" Asin said with a shrug. She eyed Tevfik, recalling the first time they had met again when she went shopping on the second day, his attention drawn to the minor commotion she had caused. In a human enchanter's shop there where her inability to speak had angered the owner. It was Tevfik who had introduced her to Mulla. And after that, well, it would have been rude to turn down his offer of dinner.

127

"*Did you think about what I said?*" Tevfik said softly as the pair walked to their favorite restaurant. One that cooked proper Beastkin food – meat wrapped in bread with more meat and spices.

"*Yes. No,*" Asin said, shaking her head. Tevfik had offered to help her sell some of the Mana Stones on the black market, one run by fellow Beastkin friends. Not too many of course, it would have been too obvious if they stopped bringing in Stones.

"*Why?*"

"*My friends trust me. Would be wrong,*" Asin said.

"*You're not taking from them. You can just cut them in on other things, make up the difference later,*" Tevfik said. "*That's what I do with my party. I even add a little. You know the government sells stones to us at one and a half times the going rate. This is just a little rebalancing.*"

"*No,*" Asin said, shaking her head. While Tevfik was right, and she did know that, it was also true that if she was caught doing something like this, the entire team would be affected. She could not do that to her friends.

"*Sorry*," Tevfik said immediately, bobbing his head. As they neared the busy restaurant, he pointed. "*Look, a table!*"

\*\*\*

"The tournament? It's being held in less than two weeks now. If you want to join, you should register soon," Nicole said to Daniel and Omrak. The guild master had found the pair seated by themselves and promptly sat down along with a pair of young ladies that had accompanied her. One, a female wearing a blouse and afghan ensemble sat next to Daniel, the other, a tall, rangy redhead had taken a seat next to Omrak, leaving Nicole to sit between the two youngsters. After the initial awkwardness, Nicole's social skills and the plying of alcoholic courage had relaxed everyone.

"But what is it going to be? Puzzles? Skill displays? An arena fight?" Daniel persisted in asking.

"Oh, arena fight," Nicole said. "For the noobs, you'll be fighting captured monsters. If you checked the Quest section, you'd see the Questors all running around cackling and exhausted by the sheer number of capture quests they've received."

"We're fighting monsters?" Daniel frowned, not expecting that.

"Of course, you are. You're Adventurers. That's what we do!" Nicole said with a snort.

"Except they've got the Blue and Whites fighting each other," Emma, the afghan-wearing brunette pointed out. "It's just that they're scared you Reds might hurt each other. Not enough defensive enchantments." As she said this, Emma fiddled with a ring on her finger.

"That too! But the Guild wants you to get more practise too. Good chance to fight strange and weird things you might never get a chance to fight otherwise," Nicole said with a nod.

"This matter doth puzzle me. Surely the Dungeon Artos cannot be suitable for both those at the highest and lowest ranks of the Advanced Classes?" Omrak said.

"Gods, I love the way you talk," mooned the redhead, Sara, as she leaned into Omrak's big arms. Flushing again, Omrak stared straight ahead.

"Artos is special. It's a third Dungeon that's sealed off most times which is why most people even forget that it's part of the city. Lots of Adventurers come and go without ever entering it. It's not a very big Dungeon either, normally. Getting into it requires you to use a portal, one that has a moonstone key on it. You can set which floor you enter with Artos," Nicole explained. "Because the portal only works for a limited number of teams, we have to limit it. But each team has to clear their floor. If not, the next time it opens, we get a Dungeon break."

"And that's why the tournament," Daniel said. "To find the best."

"Exactly."

"Nope," Emma said at the same time.

"Emma…"

"Oh, come on; you know it's bullshit. They could just use the average payout as a guide to see which team is the best at each Level. Maybe with a little judgement included for those teams that are just coming off injuries. But they don't," Emma said. "Why do you think that, huh? It's for the gold. The tournament is a great gold maker for the Guild and royal family. It's also why all the winners get prizes."

"That's ummm...." Daniel started and stopped, not sure how to respond.

"Yeah, fine. Call me crazy. Everybody does, but I'm right," Emma said with a snap, crossing her arms and pouting.

"I didn't..."

"Just leave her be, Daniel," Nicole said, shooting an unhappy look at Emma. "She's just angry. But she is right about one thing. There are prizes for winning, and the experience is well worth it. You'll find that you'll learn a lot, whether you win or lose."

"And our chances of winning?" Daniel asked curiously.

"Very low," Emma snapped. "You're Reds. Unless you're top of your category, there's no chance you're winning."

"Oh..." Daniel sighed.

"Ah, but our trainers said we were close to passing to Orange," Omrak said proudly. At this, Sara cooed, making Omrak blush slightly, but less so this time.

"Well, if you register now, you've got two weeks to prepare. Most of the teams involved have already started slowing down their delving. No one

132

wants to get hurt before the tournament," Nicole said, looking pointedly at Daniel.

"That's another reason why the tournament is a bad idea. Lets the monsters build up," Emma muttered softly, ignored by the majority. Still, Daniel heard and made a note – expect more and more monsters as they neared the start of the tournament.

# Chapter 6

"And that's it. You're registered," Seth said, tapping the form in front of him. "The group of DAO is now part of the listings for the first category. You know you'll be matched up against tougher monsters the more you fight, right?"

"We do," Daniel said.

"Good. Then my job here really is done," Seth said. "On that note, I hear your group found the way downstairs yesterday?"

"Yes. We're actually here to ask about it," Daniel said with slight trepidation.

"An Adventurer prepared today is an adventurer alive tomorrow," Seth said with a smile. "One silver each."

The trio quickly made their payments before they were, to Daniel and Omrak's chagrin, ushered off to see Quinn. Asin, sensing their hesitation, looked between the two but followed after. After all, what else could she do?

\*\*\*

"You're trying the second floor of Porthos already, eh?" Mateo said with a smile as he looked over the trio. Even as he was speaking, his hands were sweeping over the tower shield and rockbow that the party had returned, testing for problems with experienced hands.

"Yes. We got the briefing from Quinn already," Daniel said.

"And what did you think of it?" Mateo questioned.

"Caves. Small arms. Karlak," Asin said with her usual terseness.

"That's, umm... true," Mateo said, slightly bewildered by the Catkin. "It is a cave system, so I guess your experience in Karlak would help somewhat. What else?"

"Hellhounds. Single, dual and triple-head for the floor Champion. Breathe fire, so we'll have to be careful and use our Salamander cloaks," Daniel said. "Four legs, fast moving, caltrops and bolas."

"Do you all speak like that?" Mateo said with a half-smile. "But yes, you're correct again. Next."

"Lights," Omrak replied. "There are no lights."

"Correct again. So, what's that mean?" Mateo said.

"We need light," Omrak said simply.

136

"And…?"

"We carry it."

Stifling a groan, Mateo turned to Daniel who answered. "Two things. The hellhounds see in the dark, so any light we bring will bring them to us. In addition, we won't want to be fighting the hellhounds with one of our hands carrying lanterns."

"Correct," Mateo said. "Lanterns filled with oil when fire-breathing monsters are around are a bad idea too. Now, did you miss anything else?"

The trio stared at each for a moment as they cudgelled their brains. Once they all shook their heads, Mateo sniffed.

"Well, you were doing well," Mateo said mock-sadly. "But you forgot the traps. Specifically, the rock falls."

"Those…" Daniel shuddered at Mateo's words. That was a particularly nasty trap, one that the ex-Miner would probably have nightmares about.

"They're not like real mine rockfalls. They're set-up by the Dungeon, so they aren't as dangerous because it only releases a limited number of rocks,"

137

Mateo said. "Mana made rocks, which disappear after a while."

"They disappear?" Daniel said with surprise.

"Of course. How else would the passageways get cleared?"

"Ummm... workers?"

"We're no Basic dungeon with basic workers. Sure, we have Farmers enough on the first few floors, but the Guild doesn't have enough money to pay Advanced Adventurers to clear rockfalls. Even in Karlak, your people mined the Crawler spit for a reason," Mateo said. "No, the rocks are imbued with Mana to stay around when connected to the ceiling. When they fall, they lose that connection and breakdown."

"So, theoretically, someone could survive until it disappeared?" Omrak said.

"Har. If you can hold your breath for a few hours, certainly," Mateo said. "You can either buy single-use Mana disruption potions from Alchemists or rent some Mana disruption wands from us. Their uses are limited to cases like this, but it could save your lives."

"How much?" Asin asked, getting straight to the point.

138

"Deposit is ten gold coins. Rental is one per week," Mateo replied.

All three Adventurers winced at that. Still, even without the wands, the group found themselves purchasing a few useful items from the Adventurer's Store like metal caltrops that were linked to a central metal ball. It was more expensive but ensured that the team could just collect the caltrops after use easily rather than leaving them around for an unfortunate team to walk on later. An act that could result in fines if they were determined to be the culprits.

In addition, glow stones were purchased, Mana stones that had simple runes inscribed on them to draw upon the ambient Mana to power. They were utterly useless outside of a Mana-rich environment, but perfect for Dungeon delving. Daniel, of course, did not need to buy one since he had his own enchanted stone that just required repeated recharging via Mana. Sewn and attached to clothing, the glow stones gave off enough weak light in totality to allow Adventurers to watch where they were going in a pinch. And, as their last purchase, the group purchased a much more expensive Mana Lantern. This one used a Mana stone the size of the Floor Champion, the runes inscribed not on the stone itself but on the lantern, drawing upon the stone's source of power to illuminate the surroundings. Lastly, they purchased a single bottle of Mana dissolution liquid each.

All in all, the team spent all their saved earnings over the last week to just equip themselves for the next floor. It was a depressing state of affairs, one that Adventurers the world over understood. To make more gold, you needed to go to lower floors. To get to lower floors, you needed better equipment. To get better equipment, you needed to spend gold. And so, the circle continued in a never-ending fashion. Even those who decided to farm specific floors had to pay upkeep and maintenance while watching their Level growth stagnate.

\*\*\*

*Dark.* That was the first thought that crossed Daniel's mind as the group exited the Portal. Stepping aside to allow other groups to come through unmolested, Daniel waited in the safe room while the glow lights attached around his body began to draw upon the ambient Mana to power themselves. Luckily, even without his own glow lights working, the safe zone had a few scattered points of illumination to greet arrivals that gave off just a little illumination.

Asin, unlike Daniel and Omrak, had chosen to go without the illumination of the glow stones, preferring to rely on her greater sensitivity to light and the ambient amount shed by her friends. As such, while Daniel and Omrak let their eyes and stones adjust, she crept ahead. In the dark, the pair waited for their friend to return.

"Blocked," Asin said after a long time, pointing to two tunnels leading from the chamber in quick succession.

"Don't do that!" Daniel snapped, only now recovering from his surprise as the black-furred Catkin appeared next to him. Asin's only answer was a wide grin.

"Right then. We go with that one?" Daniel said, pointing. There were five exits from the portal chamber, many of which were known to be

141

blocked at any time. Even without an Adventurer to trigger them, the Dungeon occasionally released these rockfalls, altering the map of the floor. It was theorised that it was due to the Dungeon's actual inability to host more than a set number of such traps rather than a programmed design. But again, like many things dealing with the Dungeon creation, it was pure speculation.

Asin just shrugged, obviously not having more of a clue than Daniel. After a quick consultation of the map that Omrak held, the trio headed out. The floor itself was a strange one with the entrance placed almost centrally on the map. Routes through the dungeon crisscrossed one another, sometimes leading to dead-ends while other times, rock falls would block off established routes, forcing parties to chart a new path. To make the floor more challenging, to exit the floor to the next one, Adventuring groups had to collect a total of five different unlocking gems. With a full collection of gems, a party of five could transport down. Since the gems were soulbound to their owners, there was a small but persistent market of Adventurers tagging on with smaller groups to travel down a floor.

"Asin, don't go too far," Daniel called out worriedly as he once again lost sight of the Catkin. For now, the trio had decided to attempt the floor using just the smaller glow stones. The smaller stones shed less light, allowing them to stay better hidden in the darkness, but it was difficult to see. While Daniel had shown the group how to attach the stones to their helmets and adjust their illumination with some simple twisted metal, his Miner tricks might not be as useful in a fight. Certainly, Karlak never had that same issue with it's Mana imbued walls.

"I hate caves," grumbled Omrak behind Daniel as he squeezed his way through a particularly narrow passage. Even in the larger passages, the big Northerner often found himself uncomfortably tight. In these narrow passages, his arms and shoulders and chest were rubbed raw as he forced himself past them. At times, the group would have to get on their hands and knees to crawl, though none of the passages would require crawling on their bellies. It seemed even Panqua had limits on the level of suffering he would inflict on Advanced Adventurers.

"I understand," Daniel said, grumbling softly as he spotted the agile and flexible Catkin disappear ahead of him now that the pair had caught up. From past experience, Daniel had chosen to leave the majority of his plate mail pieces at home to allow him to squeeze past obstacles easier.

Their first battle was an hour into their delve. Asin, ranging ahead to check for traps, was targeted, the Hellhounds pouncing on her from the cavern niches they had been resting in. With barely enough room to swing her knives, the Catkin could only scramble backwards as she fended off the quartet of beasts, yowling for help.

"Asin!" Daniel called out, rushing forwards, his shield held before him. At first, he could only see the occasional glimpse of a blade, the flash of wide green eyes and malevolent red ones. Then, fire. Squinting in pain as a Hellhound breathed fire on Asin, Daniel continued his mad rush as the Beastkin yelped.

Luckily, the Salamander cloaks the trio sported absorbed the majority of the flames as Asin pulled it up protectively. The cloaks themselves were a necessary purchase for Karlak,

144

and so luckily all three of them had their own. Rather than actual Salamander skin, the cloaks were made of a woven, dense material that shed flame and heat with ease.

Unfortunately, the attacks by the hellhounds, and some less than stellar patching from before, meant that there were gaps - gaps which allowed flames to lick against exposed fur and skin. Falling to the ground, Asin quickly rolled back and forth in an attempt to douse the flames. A move that left her vulnerable to the bites and claws of the Hellhounds.

Leaning into his shield, his eyes still watering from the sudden shift in intensity, Daniel barrelled forwards into the group. Unable to tell when to trigger his Skill, he could only use his forward momentum and greater weight to bash aside the monsters. The impact of first one then another monster on his shield robbed Daniel of his momentum, sending him skidding on the ground as he attempted to keep his balance. His flailing arms manage to accidentally smack aside another Hellhound, the beasts now turning to focus on him.

"I got you!" Daniel said, snarling his support to Asin as he swung the hammer and shield around, spinning in space as he sought out the monsters. The creatures slunk back, two of them crouching low as they readied their flames.

"Nay, me!" roared Omrak, issuing his **Challenge of the North**. Even Daniel turned to stare at the giant Northerner who was framed by the glowing red fires of incipient flame from the hellhounds. Blond hair that had escaped from his helmet reflected the red of the flames while the hatchets in his hands glinted with challenge, the Northerner grinning widely with battle fervor. "Come!"

Fire. Both Hellhounds unleashed it against Omrak. Omrak, in turn, had lifted a corner of the cloak, hiding his face and part of his body from the flames even as it swirled around him. A third Hellhound was on the ground, choking as Asin extracted her knife from its throat, lightning arcing around its body as the Catkin extracted her revenge from it. The last Hellhound raced through the dying flames in time to launch itself at Omrak's throat the moment the Northerner lowered his arms.

"My turn," Daniel snarled and stepped forwards, swinging his helmet underhand. He engaged **Perin's Blow** the moment he struck, sending the Hellhound flying into its friend as Daniel's attack crushed its ribs. Stepping forwards, Daniel used the edge of his shield next on the struggling creature's face, triggering a **Shield Bash** to stun the monster. With the pair of Hellhounds on the ground and unable to stand, he proceeded to pummel the creatures mercilessly.

Omrak, surprised by the Hellhound's sudden attack was unable to dodge the creature's jaws. Falling on his back, the monster savagely mauled his neck, but the gorget around his throat protected it from serious damage. Still, blood spilled, shrouding the Northerner in red as he proceeded to punch the creature in the face with one hand while holding it by the ear in the other. Soon enough, the giant's overwhelming strength – aided by his Skill **Lesser Strength** – stunned the beast, allowing Omrak to roll it off him with ease and continue to attack it, this time with his hatchet. Blood flew, splashing warm against Omrak's burnt skin before the creature slowly burst apart into motes of blue light.

"Omrak!" Daniel called as he walked over, having already cast **Healer's Mark** on Asin and repeating the process when his friend finally made his way over for Daniel to touch.

"My apologies, Hero Daniel! I was caught on an outcropping," Omrak said grumpily, his eyes frowning. "How did this happen?"

"Ambush," Asin said, picking up the various Mana stones. She limped forward, her thigh bandaged from where she had been mauled. Even under the spell, it was still bleeding slightly.

"I think we should stick closer together," Daniel said, frowning around.

"Yes," Asin said quietly, slumping into a corner after a moment as the pain overtook her stubbornness. Daniel grimaced, placing a hand on her for a second to assess her damage before he decided to cast a **Minor Healing (II)** on her. Better to be safe than sorry.

***

Time passed quickly as the trio made their way in. The Hellhounds continued to launch attacks, sometimes giving ample warning as they charged down the passageways, howling their enmity. At these times, caltrops and bolas were put to use, the monsters forced to break their mad-rush and pick their way in closer to use their short-range flame attacks. On the way in, Asin's and Omrak's thrown weapons would make the hounds bleed, Daniel timing his attacks and charges to disrupt those who attempted to burn them. Against monsters who announced their presence, the trio dealt well.

It was the ones who lay in ambush, who waited in darkened alcoves above the tight passageways or crouched low in smaller passages hidden in the rocks that the trio found themselves fighting for their lives. At times, these monsters would launch their attacks before slinking away, harrying the Adventurers rather than attempting to end the fight. After the second such attack, the trio agreed to start using the larger lantern, allowing Omrak to carry it aloft to illuminate their surroundings better. With its use and reflection, the trio found themselves beset more but less prone to ambushes.

Having had experience dealing with caverns, the trio had packed for a long period in the underground. It was not the monsters that were the greatest challenge but the environment. Occasionally, the party would run into others, often in natural chokepoints. Here, groups would have to wait for others to pass through the latest obstacle, often in single file. Whether it was a particularly tight hole, a wall that had to be climbed or an extremely narrow passage, parties would often gather in such spots. At such times, other parties would take advantage of the presence of others to rest, catching fitful sleep or cooking meals.

It was at one such cavern, one where a small pool of water collected and required Adventurers to wade through that the party ran into an acquaintance of sorts.

"You're Daniel and Asin aren't you?" the smiling, muscular blond said to them. He was, Daniel thought jealously, traditionally handsome. A sharp jaw, well-sculpted eyebrows and a flashing smile along with a perfectly symmetrical face and a slim but muscular body, barely hidden by the armor he wore graced the speaker.

"Yes. How did you know?" Daniel asked.

"Not many Catkin and Guidong natives around this part. I'm Bartosz," he replied, offering his hand.

Daniel frowned, standing up and shaking it. "Daniel as you know. And that's Asin and Omrak."

"Ah, Omrak." Bartosz next shook the other two's hands, exclaiming at the end as he eyed the Northerner. "You must be a new addition. Niko didn't mention you."

"Niko." Daniel's lips compressed as he stared at Bartosz. Of course, the little green robin emblem on his chest should have told Daniel where his alliance lay. "He spoke of us?"

"Mentioned you to those of us working the lower floors," Bartosz said, gesturing back to his party who were busy cooking a meal. "Care to join us?"

"Certainly," Omrak nodded his head quickly before he strode over without hesitation. "I have some beef to add to the pot!"

"Omrak…" Daniel started and sighed. Already, the friendly Northerner was chatting with the group, the roast in his hand.

"Don't worry. We aren't trying to recruit you. Niko just mentioned you two as friendly," Bartosz said and then, glancing around to make sure no one else was around, added. "You'll find that not every guild is that friendly. Too much competition you know."

"I do," Daniel said, still wary. To his surprise, Asin stared at Bartosz for a moment before stalking over to join Omrak. Daniel frowned, wondering why the change of heart – after all, she had been extremely angry at Tevfik before. Still, with both his friends at the cooking stove, it would be churlish of him to refuse the invitation.

"What are you cooking?"

"Meat and bread," Bartosz said with a shrug. "The usual. I think Reka is adding some onions to it today, and jojo shoots."

"Sounds like you're a bit tired of that," Daniel said.

152

"We've been down here for three days now. And that's all everyone thought to bring," Bartosz made a face. "I like meat. And bread. But after so many days…"

Daniel chuckled, slapping Bartosz on the shoulder. Already, Daniel could smell the spices that Asin had drawn from her stash, the chili and peppers likely to liven up the meal. If it didn't kill them. In either case, friends, even friends with agendas, would be useful down here.

# Chapter 7

"Surprised to see you here," Seth said, eyeing Daniel who had arrived early in the morning. The young man was just wearing his breastplate, though as always, he carried his shield and hammer with him. "Thought you'd be focused on the second floor."

"We just came back from our second delve. Five days in the Dungeon is a bit much," Daniel said with a grimace. They'd spent a few hours just adjusting to the greater light outdoors yesterday when they exited, squinting like old men.

"Har," Seth said, shaking his head. "Well, good choice not to go in anyway. You might not get back out before the tournament."

"That's the other reason," Daniel said and glanced back at the extremely crowded training yards. Unlike most times, the training yard beside the Adventurers Guild was packed. Since the yard was subsidised for registered Adventurers, newer and cheaper Adventurers made use of their services while more experienced Adventurers would often hire private trainers or visit one of the many private training grounds. "Busy today."

"Busy week," Seth said with a shrug. "Who do you want to see?"

"Angie, if she's free?"

"Angie?" Seth said, eyes wide in surprise. "You mean one-eyed Angie? You sure?"

"Yes, that Angie," Daniel said. "Is there another one?"

"No. Huh, you're one of those," Seth said. "One silver. And she's free."

Daniel shook his head in surprise as he paid the coin and was directed to Angie. The muscular trainer was standing next to one of the training grounds where she was heckling the trainees within. Daniel had to hide a slight smile, her constant comments about their lack of fitness, agility and common sense were humorous. To him at least.

"Angie?" Daniel called when he was closer.

"Oh, shit, I'll pay you… oh, hey. You're that Healer guy!" Angie said, the look of concern wiped from her face. "What are you doing here?"

"Training," Daniel said as he held up her chit. Angie's eye widened slightly before she broke into a grin.

"Har! I knew you were smart. Come on; we'll leave these two losers alone," Angie said with a sniff. Their trainer, an older man who had a shield

156

and sword propped near his feet, shot Daniel a grateful look before he turned back to his students. With Angie leaving, they began to slack off which made the trainer start shouting.

"Where are we going?" Daniel asked.

"To find a spot to practise, of course," Angie said with a sniff. "So, I beat you into learning how to grapple eh?"

"Well, I'd like to learn how not to lose so much," Daniel said with a grimace.

"Well, there isn't much I can teach you in such a short time, but we'll at least lay the foundation," Angie said, rubbing her chin. Having found an out of the way spot, she pointed to Daniel next. "Strip."

"Huh? I-"

"Your armor, stupid. Unless you like bruises," Angie said. Daniel flushed slightly but complied while Angie continued to speak. "Right, I should tell you some things. Firstly, what I'm going to teach you is most effective against humanoids at first. I'm also going to teach you principles, ideas and concepts mostly, rather than specific moves. It'll take you longer to learn, but it means once you get it, you can start using some of these skills against monsters."

"Monsters?" Daniel said, frowning.

"Yup," Angie said with a grin. "Like joint locks. Don't care if it's a hound, a Qimm or a Kobold, if it has a joint, it moves in a certain direction. You just need to know which way to hurt them. Oh yeah, should go without saying. Don't grapple slimes, oozes, jellyfish and their like."

"People have tried that?" Daniel said, trying to imagine how that'd go. The mind boggled.

"I've had some dumb students," Angie said matter of factly.

"Oh," Daniel said quietly, unsure where to go from there.

"Since you're a Healer, I'm going to skip my usual spiel about joints, tendons, nerves and the like. Now, give me your hand…" Angie continued on, ignoring the awkwardness of the situation as she strode over to Daniel. Warily, Daniel extended his hand and she grabbed it, pulling him towards her quickly and twisting it. "Now, the first thing you want to do when you grapple is take their balance. Unbalanced individuals lack a base which means they can't generate as much strength to hit you. Of course, if they've got claws, are elementals or have spikes, that's a less of a concern for them. But…"

***

Hours later, Daniel sat on the ground, groaning softly. Angie had been relentless, her philosophy being that something felt was more easily learned than something spoken. As such, with each joint manipulation, each lock, each imparted piece of wisdom, she demonstrated on Daniel. Of course, once she got past the basics, she let Daniel test out the movements on her body. But it still left Daniel sore and hurting, especially since Angie's most common refrain was, "Suck it up or heal yourself. Now come on, do that again." After which, when Daniel failed to properly lock her down, she'd escape and show him a new and innovative way to make him eat dirt.

"So, I know we've been having fun, but that silver was only for two hours," Angie said leadingly as she sat on a chair, swigging from a flask. Even from here, Daniel could smell the red wine that it contained.

"Sorry. I'll pay Seth later," Daniel said. "Or I could-"

"Nah, if you say you're good for it, I believe you."

Daniel nodded his thanks, glad that he could just wait for his body to stop aching. Unbeknownst to Angie, he had tapped into his Gift slightly rather than a spell like she had expected. Mostly to fix torn muscles and twisted joints, boosting their healing speed. The sore muscles and exhaustion he left alone.

"How come-" Daniel started and then stopped, unsure if it was impolitic to continue further.

"How come I don't have more students?" Angie said and sighed. "Most people, they'd rather hit things. And they figure they can just hit things till a friend comes along to save them. Maybe they'd come over for a few lessons to learn some escapes. A few ways to get out and back up, but mostly? It's bash, bash, bash."

"Ah," Daniel said with a grimace. That was after all what he had come here to learn too.

"It's okay. I get it. At your level, most of your skills are weapon based. Hard to use a **Cleave** without a sword. Or a **Shield Bash** without a shield," Angie said. "You got to go with where your Skills are. But, you know, with a little more training, when you're getting up? You could break a limb or two, take the bastard down. Keep them from hurting you or your friend."

"How much more training?" Daniel said with a frown. That sounded... reasonable.

"A couple of months," Angie said. "For a humanoid. Maybe a few more to get comfortable enough to use it against non-humanoids."

"Oh..." Daniel said, pausing as he considered her words. He was only twenty-two this year, so spending half a year studying a series of skills that was only marginally useful seemed intimidating. Then again, it was a skill he would need, might need for the rest of his, hopefully, long career.

"Well, you done resting?" Angie said, bouncing back to her feet as she pushed aside any doubt. "We got more to learn today. If you've got the money for it, that is."

"I do," Daniel said with a nod. Over in the corner, Daniel noted that Omrak was also training, having arrived an hour ago to study how to wield his sword better. They had only a few days left for the tournament after all.

\*\*\*

The last few days passed in a haze of training. Daniel would stumble back to their inn, exhausted to take his meal from Erin's waiting hands. Sometimes alone, sometimes with his friends, Daniel would consume multiple portions of the meal in silence before stumbling upstairs to sleep. It was only because the Guild had bathhouses that he was at all presentable, his exhaustion so great that Daniel would never have thought of making his way to another building.

To Daniel's astonishment, somehow, Omrak always managed to stay up later than him, spending at least a few hours longer in the common room, drinking and otherwise partying with newfound friends. Even with the attractive prizes offered by the tournament, not all parties took part, preferring to save their coin and take advantage of the quieter floors to complete Quests and their exploration.

Asin, on the other hand, was even more enigmatic, spending her days training away from the Guild. When questioned, she just indicated she had found a training location in the Beastkin district. Daniel, noting her reluctance to speak, left the matter alone even as curiosity gnawed at him.

Still, the day before the tournament started, all three were seated in the crowded inn. Many of the other Adventurers intent on joining the tournament were taking the day off as well, content to let their bodies heal and not daring to risk a minor injury the day before the event. It ensured that Erin and her workers were extremely busy that day, running to fill orders. Even if Daniel could heal their bodies, he could do nothing about their mind, and so the team too took the day off – they had spent the entirety of the last few weeks doing their best to catch up, after all.

"How did you all do?" Daniel asked curiously.

"I leveled up my two-handed weapons skill," Omrak said proudly, grinning. "You see before you a Novice 4 two-handed sword wielder."

163

"Nice," Daniel said. "That'll give you more options the next time you gain a Level, right?"

"Yes," Omrak nodded. "I am curious to see what options are available. It would have to be extremely attractive to take me away from **Cleave,** however."

"Har," Daniel chuckled. He knew that Omrak had been lusting over the powerful single strike attack for a while. He would have taken it before, but the need for a crowd control ability had taken precedence for the party. It was a sacrifice that Daniel fully appreciated. "Well, we'll find out."

"Yes, we will," Omrak said, then grinned. "We might just Level in the tournament."

"Maybe." Daniel shrugged. The introduction of new monsters normally gave fighters a boost to their experience which was part of why the tournament was so popular. Of course, normally was the important word. If an Adventurer did not gain enough experience from fighting it – whether due to a quick battle or just a lack of perception – they would not gather that bonus. "Asin?"

"Leveled. New Skill. **Bone breaker,**" Asin said.

"You gained a Level?" Daniel said, surprised.

"Close. Dungeon. Friend," Asin said with a shrug.

"Really, a friend took you to the Dungeon," Daniel said again slowly. "Who we haven't met."

"Jealous?" Asin asked, her ears shifting and tail now straight up behind her. Daniel frowned, reading the displeasure in her tail and paused, considering her words. Why was she angry?

"No. Not jealous. Just worried," Daniel said slowly, considering his own roiling emotions. "And surprised. Never thought you'd keep a friend like that to yourself."

Asin sniffed slightly at Daniel's word, her nose wrinkling. The silence stretched but slowly, her tail relaxed and started waving again. In the end, ducking her head into the mug, she said one more word, quietly. "Tevfik."

"Tevfik!?!" Daniel exclaimed then lowered his voice, embarrassed. Not that anyone heard, the numerous conversations around them drowning out his own exclamation. "Sorry. Just surprised."

"What is Tevfik?" Omrak asked, turning to stare at his two friends.

"Oh. Hmmm…" Daniel paused, realising that the pair had left the Catkin out of their stories about Silverstone. After all, Tevfik was more a personal matter than a Dungeon matter. "He was Asin's ummm… boyfriend?"

"Boyfriend," Asin replied with a firm nod. "Is."

"Oh. You're back together. Of course, you are," Daniel said, shaking his head. A niggle of worry rose up in him, concerned that his young friend was getting in over her head again. Recalling how her father had *suggested* that he keep an eye on his daughter in Karlak, Daniel could not help but worry for her. When Asin glared at him, he ducked his head and just made a note to keep an eye on this.

"Congratulations!" Omrak said, clapping Asin on the shoulder and nearly knocking the slender Catkin off her chair. She snarled at Omrak who just laughed.

"You?" the Catkin said and then leaned in, sniffing slightly. "Sara?"

"Nothing happened!" Omrak said, almost jumping in his seat as he hastily spoke. "Nothing. We're just talking."

166

"You know she wants to do more than talk, right?" Daniel said, his lips tugging upwards slightly.

"This…" Omrak flushed and then stared straight at Daniel as he changed the topic. "What did you learn?"

"It's okay to talk about these things you know, it's perfectly natural - especially for us Adventurers," Daniel said, eyes glinting with humor.

"What. Did. You. Learn."

Chuckling softly, Daniel dropped the topic. "I spent the last few days learning grappling – unarmed combat really – with Angie."

Both his friends frowned slightly at Daniel who snorted, "I'm not stupidly strong or agile like some people. This gives me more options when I'm on my back. My Unarmed Combat skills progressed because of it along with my Combat Sense."

With that said, the group fell silent. In the end, it was Omrak who broached the subject that was on all their minds. "Can we win?"

"We'll find out tomorrow," Daniel replied.

Asin too shrugged before waving to the waitress and took the three mugs of ale from her. Quickly paying the waitress who was already on the way back to the bar, Asin lifted her mug to her friends.

"Victory."

"Victory!" The pair cheered with her, draining their mug. Whatever happened tomorrow, at least it would be interesting, thought Daniel.

# Chapter 8

To keep things running smoothly, and to ensure the tournament would be over in time, the battles for the lowest tier parties were being held first. This would allow the largest number of contestants to be run through the arena as quickly possible. The battles were also planned this way to ensure that the Adventurers had enough time to heal from minor injuries before entering Artos if they won.

As such, the trio found themselves amongst a large group of other parties, each eyeing the competition warily. A few groups, disregarding the tension, spoke with one another happily, grouping in distinct clumps. Most of these groups were older, with better equipment and held badges for the larger guilds in town.

It was not really surprising to Daniel. If the team had not rushed the first floor, it could easily take any other party a few good months to clear fully, especially if you included injury and recovery time. Many groups would rarely progress to the next Level immediately, even if they could, eking out as much of their gains as possible. The second floor, as Daniel and team had found out, would be even more difficult. Even with their advantages, Daniel did not expect them to clear the Dungeon floor in less than three months. That was with, what Daniel considered, ample time to rest – but he also knew that their party had a work ethic that few other parties seemed to hold. Too many Adventurers were content to earn enough for a few months fun and rest before taking a break. Perhaps it was because Daniel had been forced to wait so long that he felt the ever-present rush of time.

"Welcome, everyone," a loud voice called as a man in a waistcoat and with a cane stood on a box that had been laid out for him. "My name is Jules Sherred. I'll be the ringmaster and announcer today. Firstly, thank you for arriving early. In a moment my people will begin allocating all of you to your respective waiting rooms. Due to the number of parties involved, we're going to have you fighting in groups of five. The first round will be a timed event. If you fail to defeat your monsters in the five minutes allocated, you will not move on to the second round."

Jules fell silent, content to let the murmuring grow for a bit before he raised his hand. Whether it was skill or a Skill, he received silence a moment later. "I understand your concerns, but our space and time are limited. Depending on the number of groups that pass the first round, we might have to undertake an elimination format for the second. Once we have reached an acceptable number of parties, we will begin a point style progression where the groups with the highest number of kills and clears will be chosen to enter Artos."

Once more, grumbling began, but this time Jules did not signal for it to end. Instead, Jules jumped off the box and disappeared back into the arena. In a moment, clerks streamed out from the arena, all carrying stylised stone boards in hand. When the clerk finally reached their group, Daniel noted that these stone boards were inscribed with enchantments.

"Team?"

"DAO," Omrak answered.

The clerk flicked his finger along the board, names appearing and disappearing as the enchantment altered the display. Having found their entry, the clerk said, "Room C8. Go in, turn left and enter the third – that's third – passageway you come across on your right. Now, repeat that back to me."

"Room C8. Left and then the third right passageway," Daniel said. Without a word, the clerk turned and walked away, leaving the trio.

"I guess we have our marching orders," Daniel said, gesturing for the team to go in.

Together, the trio entered the arena, walking through its Mana stone-lit stone corridors with other teams in silence. Now that they were in the arena itself, the tension increased, each group growing quieter as they walked to their rooms. It was an unpleasant, if not entirely unexpected, surprise to find that they would be sharing the room with three other groups. Taking their own corner, the party quietly got settled.

Within the hour, the team could hear the muffled thread and the muted conversations of the audience as they entered the arena. Even located beneath the arena as they were, the noise and movement reverberated through the room. It was no surprise; the arena had purposely priced the first day of the tournament at an extremely low price to not only provide the parties exposure but to fill the stadium. After all, compared to the Blue and White Advanced Adventurers, the fights that were to be showcased would be significantly less of a draw.

In another two hours, the first roars from the crowd could be heard as the event started. By this time, many of the groups had taken to sitting down and busying themselves as their personalities dictated. All around the trio, Adventurers were reading, snacking, repeatedly sharpening and caring for weapons and, in one group's case, having a raucous good time playing cards. Asin was busy juggling her knives while Omrak watched, cleaning his sword. Daniel himself had taken to reading, perusing a book on herbal products and their uses as he worked to expand his own knowledge of healing. Yet, for all his discipline, Daniel found himself re-reading the same page again and again.

"When is it going to be our turn?" Daniel said as he placed his finger in the book.

There were a few grunts of agreement at Daniel's exasperated exclamation, but soon enough silence took over. And still, they waited.

***

"Come on, Omrak," Daniel said, his growing annoyance layering his words.

"Mmmpphhfffblrgh!" Omrak muttered, swigging on his canteen as the trio hurried out onto the arena sands. Their turn had finally come, at the most inopportune moment as the trio had begun to eat lunch. Rather than set the food aside, Omrak had stuffed the meat pastry into his mouth as they rushed after the clerk.

It was to this sight – that of a giant blond Northerner, cheeks stuffed with food and carrying a mighty two-handed sword lead by a Catkin in a short cloak and a fully clad, iron plate mail-wearing Adventurer - that greeted the audience. The roars of excitement died down slightly as the crowd took in this strange sight, especially when Daniel's footsteps stuttered and stopped as he walked in.

So many people. That was all that the young Adventurer could think of. Omrak seemed to glow under the attention of the crowd, straightening his back and waving to everyone while Asin ignored it all as she focused on the other side of the stadium. Around them, only the slightest shimmer of blue indicated that they were magically walled off from the other groups in the sandy arena, some of who were engaged in desperate battle.

"… triumvirate, DAO!" Jules' voice roared, somehow piercing the roar of the crowd. "And facing them is… well, you guessed it. Kobolds!"

"Daniel!" Asin hissed, her tail slapping the young man's face. Daniel blinked as he refocused, pushing aside the crowd even as the doors rolled open and a dozen Kobolds, small, gangly looking creatures without fur and carrying daggers and crude spears came out. Unlike the Kobolds in Karlak, these monsters looked better fed and more confused.

"Kobolds. Har! This will be simple," Omrak said as he finished swallowing the last of his meal. "I shall deal with them myself." With a laugh, the big Northerner took off running, his sword held by his side.

"No…" Asin growled, shaking her head as she ran after him. Within seconds, she had overtaken the Northerner, knives already appearing in her hand as she closed to throwing distance.

Daniel grimaced, seeing that there would be no planning. Well, that was okay. There were just Kobolds. Taking up the run as well, Daniel found himself lagging behind his friends who had left without him, forcing him to try – and fail – to catch up in his plate mail.

Even as he ran, Daniel saw Asin throw her daggers, the weapons expanding as she triggered **Fan of Knives**. Kobolds ducked, blocked and otherwise scrambled out of the way of the attack, all but one unlucky monster avoiding the attack. But it had done its part, spreading the monsters to allow Omrak's reckless charge to enter their midst. With a laugh, Omrak began to swing his sword in big, looping attacks that split the Kobolds further.

Barked, guttural orders issued from the mouth of one of the larger, older looking monsters. Within seconds, the group had reconfigured itself with a trio of spear wielders suddenly facing Omrak, harassing him with their spears while the remainder split off to attack Asin and Daniel. The Kobold leader himself charged Asin, his body seeming to grow in size as he attacked her with his sword followed by the majority of the remainder.

Another pair with their own short swords focused on Daniel as he arrived.

"Thanks," Daniel growled as he hunkered beneath his shield and took the strike. Rather than slowing down, Daniel used the attack and moment's vulnerability to trigger a **Shield Bash**, the attack ripping the sword out of the smaller creature's hand. However, before he could capitalise on the moment of weakness, the other Kobold darted in with a thrust to his face.

"No, you shall **fight…**" Omrak stuttered to a stop, a glowing green spear thrust straight at his face. His attempt at invoking the **Challenge of the North** interrupted by another Skill, Omrak was forced to block the attack, leaving him open for a thrust by another spear wielder. This attack skidded off his armor, bruising the Northerner who then spun to deal with this threat.

"They're using Skills!" Daniel shouted to warn his team, eyes wide. Like Omrak, Daniel had been surprised they had chosen Kobolds to deal with the Advanced Class Adventurers, but the fact that these non-Dungeon created Kobolds could use Skills explained much. The fact that they were working together, keeping the trio apart and focusing attention on the least armored member also did as well.

"Help!" Asin shouted as she ducked another cut, her arms and torso already bleeding. Even her enchanted necklace was glowing, overworked as it was as it altered the angle of attacks at the last second as the Kobold leader pressed the group's advantage by swarming the Catkin.

"Damn it," Daniel snarled, deciding to risk it. Focusing his attacks on the second Kobold facing him, he turned his back mostly to the other and started swinging his weapon, driving his opponent back towards his comrades' encirclement of Asin.

A blow rang off his back, staggering Daniel a bit. That motion allowed his opponent in the front to jump forwards to thrust at his raised weapon arm, aiming for the unarmored space.

"Got you," Daniel slammed his shield forward, triggering **Shield Bash** and punching the monster backwards. A little too slow as the cold steel dug into his arm, leaving a long furrow. Daniel knew it would hurt later, but for now, it was a distraction. Stepping sideways, as the Kobold recovered, Daniel triggered **Perin's Blow** to send the monster crashing into Asin's encirclement.

Their line broken, the Kobolds fell back to recover. But instead of leaping away, Asin jumped forward with a snarl on her face at their leader. She blocked his reflexive attack with one knife while using the pommel of her other dagger to smash into the monster's head, triggering **Bone Breaker** at that time while lightning arced into him from her enchanted bracers. The Kobold fell backwards, stunned with a new dent on his head while Asin kept up the assault, her daggers dancing.

Snarls erupted from the Kobolds as they moved to protect their leader, but Daniel took a swift step forwards, positioning himself to block the majority as he spammed **Double Strike** to keep the Kobolds away, chasing them around. Behind, Omrak howled as he took advantage of the momentary chaos to split a Kobold apart, its corpse falling to the ground twitching before turning to deal with his other two attackers. Already, a red light shone all across his body as bleeding wounds covered his arms and trickled out from an injured shoulder.

A faked blow drew a Kobold in, close enough for Daniel to lash out with his hammer and break its arm. Another Kobold thrust its sword in the gap created by Daniel's attack, the Kobold's attack skittering along the Adventurer's armor with a shriek of metal on metal, causing Daniel to flinch. As he recovered, a third Kobold threw itself at the stocky Adventurer's leg, attempting to take him down.

A silly move, considering the disparity in size and Daniel's recent training. Hunching his body slightly to shift his weight, he took the lunge and then dropped the edge of his shield onto the Kobold's back of the head, crumpling the smaller monster. Yet, for all his heroics, Daniel could not stop the Kobolds from streaming around him to attack his friend. Still, he had bought her enough time to leave the Kobold leader on the ground, choking on its blood.

"**No more!**" roared Omrak, having speared another of his Kobold's with a lunge. His attack had earned him a spear in his leg, but with both Kobold's unable to attack, Omrak took the moment to trigger his taunt ability. At once the Kobolds all turned to the new threat, drawn by the Skill-infused challenge.

"Mine," Daniel growled as he spun his hammer into a fleeing Kobold's ribs. A second later, he lashed out again to finish the monster while Asin threw a dagger empowered with **Piercing Shot** into the back of another Kobold's body.

As the remaining Kobold's clustered around Omrak, he triggered his new ability, the red cloud of light forming into bolts of lightning that struck each of the monsters around him. Kobolds screamed in pain and in a few cases, expired from the attack, allowing the Adventurers a brief respite to finish the battle. With both the leader and their Skill-wielding brethren dead, the remaining monsters were easy to finish.

Daniel groaned as he leaned over, breathing slowly as he attempted to catch his breath. Even the smell of spilt blood, torn entrails and voided bowels were insufficient to stop him from breathing deeply. In another portion of the arena, Daniel noted a few Adventurers unable to contain themselves and were throwing up, unable to handle the gore and mess of monsters slain outside the Dungeon. Daniel quietly thanked his lucky stars that their previous experience with Quests and the war had inured their group to some extent to such displays.

"And DAO completes the first round in four minutes and twenty-three seconds," Jules announced. "Congratulations! Now clear the arena."

Even as Jules spoke, attendants were rushing out with wheelbarrows to cart away the bodies. At the pointed reminders, the trio made their way out, all three limping and moving gingerly from the fight. As they exited, Daniel could not help but overhear one last comment.

"Useless. They'll not last past the second round with those injuries."

# Chapter 9

"Die vermin! DIE!" Omrak shouted as he smashed his sword into the Poison Cockroach's back. The creature twisted and turned, its back flattening under the blow and its wings and shell cracking apart under the repeated assaults.

Next to the Northerner, Daniel busied himself with crushing the legs of another Cockroach, his shield dripping from the poison that the monsters had spat. With each leg crippled, the monster was slowed further. Already, half its legs had been smashed, one leg barely hanging on by a thread as the monster attempted to scuttle to face him.

Asin, seeing that the pair were nearly done with their monsters, ran back towards the group, jumping and spinning around to send a pair of knives shrieking through the air as she triggered **Piercing Shot.** The attacker flew through the air to harass the monsters she had led away, continuing to pull the monsters towards her. Landing, the Catkin sprinted past Omrak before she pulled to a halt, her chest heaving.

"Good job, Asin!" Daniel called as he ducked deep, taking the Cockroach's lunging bite on his shield before he pried it up higher and triggered **Perin's Blow** in an underhand strike. Lifted by the attack, the Cockroach fell over on its back to be ignored by Daniel as he scrambled to join the fight against the newly arrived, bleeding pair next to Omrak.

Too out of breath to answer, Asin just panted in the corner, her hands trembling as the poison coursed through her veins. Her dagger dropped from her numb fingers, forcing her to whimper slightly. *Stupid poison,* Asin cursed. She had dodged most of one attack, only to land and get hit by another of the monster's attacks. At least she had managed to kill one of the three she had distracted while the pair finished off their monstrosities.

As the wave of pain passed, Asin looked up to see her friends finishing off the last of the Cockroaches. Lips pursed, she drew another knife and threw it at the overturned monster, the throw plunging into the creature's soft underbelly. Yet, it did not expire, making the Catkin growl in frustration. As she fumbled for another dagger, Omrak strode over with his sword to stab it into the helpless creature and Daniel placed a hand on her.

"Hold still," Daniel muttered, casting first **Minor Healing (II)** and then **Healer's Mark**.

"Thank you. That would have been a lot harder without your distraction."

As Asin's head slowly cleared, she sniffed at herself and yowled in anger. She stank, and so did the damn arena. After three different rounds in the tournament with multiple groups using the arena, even the cleaning spells used by the staff were beginning to fail in its effectiveness.

"Spell?" Asin said after she realised that Daniel had used his magic in public. Thus far, he had been holding back till they were out of sight.

"Doesn't matter. If the crowd and our competitors haven't realised it yet, they haven't been paying attention," Daniel said, helping Asin limp back out.

Asin sighed and looked at the various body parts, tempted to dismember one of those corpses to find its poison sacks. But of course, they weren't given the time to do that. Nor the right. The corpses were the property of the arena. In fact, that was perhaps the most disappointing aspect of this tournament – the lack of Mana Stones or other earnings.

If it wasn't for the fact that she had earned a decent sum betting on their wins, Asin would have been even more upset. At the thought of the coin awaiting her in Tevfik's hand, the young Catkin's tail began to lazily sway once more. More coins…

\*\*\*

"You're only doing this well because you've got a healer," growled an Adventurer later that evening when the trio had left the arena and were seated at their table in the Lonely Candle. The arena had managed to squeeze one more fight in for the majority of groups, leaving the team with a total of four wins now. Six more battles and they would be done.

"Pardon?" Daniel said, looking up at the irate Adventurer.

"I said, you guys are cheating by having a healer in your party," the Adventurer said, spitting to the side. Daniel frowned as he stared at the man who looked to be in his early-thirties and clad in a simple studded leather tunic. A scar ran across one side of his face, down to his neck and around his arm was a fresh new bandage that still leaked a little. "You have no skill, no tactics. You all just rush in and fight!"

"Is that not our job?" Omrak said as he looked genuinely puzzled. "I fear I do not understand how else we are to defeat our opponents."

"Tactics. Long range fire, a shield wall, crowd control and damage over time attacks. Wear them down, keep yourself protected!" the scarred Adventurer almost spat the words out. "You, you! You're the worse. You just rush them and then take the hits so you can use your Skill!"

Once again, Erin appeared near the burgeoning trouble and smiled at the Adventurer. "Devin, perhaps this isn't the time? I know you're upset you have to pull out, but it's not their fault, no?"

"Bah!" Devin said as he pulled his arm away from Erin's touch. "Any other group that took the kind of damage they did would have to pull out. She just got poisoned today!" Devin said, pointing at Asin. "And here she is, happily eating away."

In reply Asin just hissed at Devin before she returned to stuffing her face. The Catkin was

187

ravenous as evidenced by the empty plates around her, the constant abuse of the healing spells over the last few days draining the Catkin's vitality. It was something that Daniel was slightly concerned about – each fight required them to be near perfect form, but even magic had its consequences.

"And I hear Maria and Vasco are both poisoned too," Erin said, sympathy in her voice. "But they'll be fine in a few days with rest."

"But we can't go in, not injured like this," Devin said with a grimace. "And we're not going to waste good healing potions on the low chance that we'll win."

"I know, I know," Erin said, once again placing her hand on the scarred Adventurer's arm and gently guiding him back to his seat. "Why don't I get you a glass of hot milk, eh? Maybe mixed with some Kowla blood for your arm?"

"Well, I do like milk…"

Omrak sat quietly, still staring at where the group had left before he turned to Daniel, his brows furrowed. "Are we cheating?"

"There are no rules saying we can't use healing spells," Daniel said firmly. "And if you haven't noticed, other groups are using healing potions too between fights."

"But…"

"We're fighting the best way we know how," Daniel said. "We could try to use more ranged weapons, but I suck at aiming. And you've got two hatchets. I'd rather be ready for when they close with us than to, maybe, kill one on the way in. And your Skill is useful."

Asin nodded at Daniel's words before adding. "No Skills. Use what we have."

"Very well," Omrak subsided, somewhat mollified. As another plate of ribs arrived, the blond giant grinned and focused on feeding his hungry body.

Even Daniel, his stomach stuffed, reached for another piece. He'd touch them all up later today with his Gift. Still, as Daniel bit into the ribs, he considered what had been said. Their trio of Adventurers was literally the smallest team on the field. Most other groups were at least five strong, sometimes as many as seven. It gave them a wider range of spells, defenses and Skills to use.

***

"What are those things?" Omrak growled as he stared at the flapping monstrosities that slowly circled higher in the arena. Finding their exit blocked by an invisible shield, the flock of monsters turned towards the Adventurers who stood watching them below.

"Shabaz according to Jules," Daniel said absently as he continued to load the crossbow he had pulled from his inventory. Stuck near his feet were a pair of other bolts, ready for his use. Though it would be a miracle if he had a chance to actually use them.

"But what do they do?" Omrak growled. The golden birds, seeming to have made a decision, tucked their wings in close and started to dive bomb the group.

"Incoming," Asin said as she scampered a distance from the pair. Omrak, seeing the sense in her actions, took steps away from Daniel too as he readied his hatchets. Now, he really wished he had that tower shield once again.

Asin's **Fan of Knives** were the first to fly out and be deflected by a pulse of golden light. The daggers, pushed away, fell around the group. Omrak's hatchet, flying in slower and a beat behind Asin, managed to escape the deflection from the first bird but was battered away by the second. Hunched behind his crossbow, Daniel waited as the birds neared, holding fire till he was certain he could hit.

As he readied himself to pull the trigger, another flash of gold occurred. Even before it finished, a second, third and fourth flash repeated in quick succession. Close to the party now, the flashes of gold forced the Adventurers to squint, their bodies rocked by the attacks. None were particularly damaging, no more than a particularly stiff punch, but one that affected their whole body no matter their armor. And it was, unfortunately, repeated till all eight birds had used their ability and started winging away.

"Damn it," Daniel cursed, his eyes still struggling to focus after the visual attacks. By the time he regained the initiative, the flock were in the sky again, getting ready to return.

"Timer," Asin snarled as she fingered her knives.

"Damn it. That's why they have this on a timer. I don't think we're expected to clear them all," Daniel said. Certainly, for their team, this would be a challenging fight.

True to his expectations, when the allocated five minutes were over, the trio had only managed to take down a single bird. Working together, the trio had timed their combined attack to start before the birds had reached the attack distance for their shield spell, forcing them the creatures to choose to waste their gifts or attempt to dodge. That Asin had hidden a last, **Piercing Shot** behind Omrak's throw had been the attack that scored the kill.

As the trio gloomily walked back to a series of boos and taunts, they could not help but reflect on their further shortcomings.

\*\*\*

Later that evening, Erin jaw dropped as she saw the three Adventurers returning from the arena, the large Northerner helped along by both his friends. His leg had been splinted and bandaged, held aloft as they walked him over to the nearest free table.

"What happened?" Erin asked, glancing down at the break. Having been an Innkeeper in Silverstone for so many years, Erin knew that such a break likely saw the end of their remarkable run. For a trio of Red ranked Advanced Adventurers to have made it this far, it was incredible. Many more experienced, larger and better-equipped parties had already fallen out of the tournament as the cumulative injuries, and the risks, kept increasing with each fight. As it stood, there was only one day left in the tournament with four fights scheduled for that day. A gruelling last day indeed. Even Erin, normally bored to such spectacles, intended to watch at least a few.

"Omrak decided to counter charge the Thyreophora," Daniel said with a shake of his head.

"It worked!" Omrak protested and grunted as Daniel dropped the Northerner on the seat not too gently.

"At the cost of your leg!" Daniel snapped. "You might have stunned it with your charge, but now you're injured."

"I just require some healing," Omrak protested.

"It's a big bone!" Daniel snapped, then drew a deep breath. "Broken bones aren't that easy to heal. The healing spells I know only set it in place a little bit. You could walk on it, but one good hit and you're done. And the next time it breaks, it could shatter."

"You could-"

Asin's claws dug into Omrak's shoulder, making the giant shut his mouth.

Erin said nothing, continuing to act oblivious to the interaction. It had been clear to her that there was more to Daniel and his healing than his self-confessed healing spells. Otherwise, it would have been impossible for the group to be as well put together as they had been. But, as an Innkeeper, it was none of her business. Adventurers always had secrets, whether it was a powerful enchantment or an artifact from ages past. The important thing was that it did not endanger the city or her inn. Everything else was none of her business.

"I'll do my best," Daniel said and then turned away, waving a hand in farewell. "I'm going to get some herbs."

"Upstairs?" Asin said, looking pleadingly at Erin who sighed. At least they ate a lot and paid without argument.

An hour later, the young healer found Erin working in the kitchen, readying the mugs and cutlery for the evening rush. Already, the inn was becoming crowded.

"Erin? I was wondering if I could get some boiling water and a pot?" Daniel said, one hand clutching a satchel of herbs.

"Of course. Darla!" Erin called and instructed the maid before she turned to Daniel. "Just wait by the bar. She'll bring it out for you."

"Thank you."

"Will you be pulling out?" Erin asked.

"I don't know yet," Daniel said, rubbing his chin. "We don't want to, but tomorrow there are four fights."

"And another break would force your friend to take a real break," Erin finished. Once again, she noted something in the youngster's eyes but declined to pursue it.

"Yes. It's a risk," Daniel muttered. "Do you think you could have her add this to the boiling water for five minutes?" He said, holding up the satchel.

"Of course," Erin picked up the herbs and walked into the kitchen. A quick, curious glance inside showed most of the usual mixture of herbs that she had come to expect. Still, Erin left, pondering that look in Daniel's eyes. Somehow, she doubted that the party would be pulling out tomorrow. Perhaps she would put a few coins on them finishing the tournament.

\*\*\*

"Hold still, you big lunk," Daniel growled as he tightened the sticks around Omrak's body. "Sticking your sword in its mouth and enraging it…"

"Do I have to drink this?" Omrak complained as the pain subsided.

"Yes. It'll help the healing process. It'll give my Gift something to pull upon too when I use it later."

"But it tastes like Roc droppings!"

"Then stop taking risks like that," Daniel snapped and then held a hand up almost immediately. "Sorry. Not fair. If you hadn't charged it and stabbed your sword in its mouth, we wouldn't have won. That armor was ridiculous."

"Apology accepted, of course, Hero Daniel. But you are unusually upset."

"Worried," Asin answered for Daniel.

"We will be fine tomorrow," Omrak said, placing a hand on Daniel's shoulder.

"Stupid. No. Gift."

"Asin is right. Using my Gift on you, well, I'm afraid some people might guess," Daniel said.

"In truth, Hero Daniel, I understand not your fear in this matter," Omrak said.

"Huh. Well, if you think the guilds have been obstinate now, if they realise what my Gift can do, they'll be even more persistent," Daniel said. "But it's not just that. Lords and ladies, rich merchants and less savory but powerful individuals – they'd all take an interest. Being able to heal almost anything…"

"Powerful," Asin said softly. "Kings. Queens. Anyone."

"Exactly," Daniel said, shadows in his eyes as he recalled his past.

"Ah. And the cost to you would be a trivial matter to them," Omrak said. Then as he glanced down at his leg, his lips tightened before he made up his mind. "Cast your healing spell. I shall strive to be more careful."

"Not happening," Daniel said, rejecting the offer immediately. "We either skip the fight and let you heal properly or we do it right. You're not going out there on a matchstick leg."

"Hero Daniel…"

"Right," Asin said, putting a hand on Omrak's shoulder and shaking her head as he tried to protest further. Omrak sighed and subsided before making a face as Asin held aloft the noxious mixture of herbs to his lips. Whichever choice was made, drinking the mixture was the correct action.

# Chapter 10

"We give up!" Daniel called immediately after the door rolled open revealing the Salamander King and its trio of guards. Even across the arena, he could feel the heat radiating from the foursome. There was nothing they had that would stop the Salamander's before they arrived and even if they equipped their cloaks, they were meant to stop sudden bursts of flames. Not the on-going, furnace level heat these creatures put out. Better to run away than die.

Behind, the doors rolled open as Daniel and team backed up. Occasional taunts erupted, but for the most part, the audience stayed silent. This was a Dungeon Town. And if most of the audience were not Adventurers, they knew someone, were related to someone, in the business. They understood the dangers that Adventuring involved and how, sometimes, the right call was the one that had you running. Still, it was good that there were other teams to watch, as the crowd turned their attention to groups who were willing enough, daring enough or just Skilled enough to take on the Salamanders.

"How many is that?" Daniel said, almost rhetorically as tamers quietly corralled the

Salamanders, pushing them back in to await the next team.

"Two," Asin replied as the trio moved back to their waiting room. The trio was glum, each thinking over the last half-day.

The first couple of fights this day had gone well. Or at least, as well as could be expected. Having brought along their nets from Karlak, the group had been able to deal with the Shadow Cats in their first battle simply enough, suffering mild injuries. Enough so that Daniel had only to cast a **Healer's Mark** on Asin. Omrak, however, had to enter the next fight injured, Daniel cautious about over-burdening the Northerner's body.

The second battle of the day was more exhausting as the group was pushed to their utmost by the Laksha – a horned, ape-like creature with wings and coarse, brown fur that provided a layer of protection on its body. The monster was, for all its six feet height, nimble and cunning. Wing sweeps would force Asin back when she attempted to backstab it, while sudden lunges and its claws tore into its target. When it felt surrounded, the monster would wing away into the sky again. It was only due to the creature's inability to stay aloft for long periods of time that allowed the team to finally take it down after a long, protracted battle.

Now, the trio were seated in the empty but for them waiting room. All the other teams had either failed, dropped out or moved to their own room. Without a word, Daniel quietly checked on all their bandages, forcing the group to drink the herbal remedies he had brought before sitting down himself. While his own wounds ached, he had quietly sealed many of the deep injuries. An advantage of understanding his own body and Gift better than any other – he could afford to fix himself with smaller consequences. And still…

*A kiss. Was it his first kiss? It was the first he could remember, but surely Lorelei had kissed him before. Or he her. There they were, hidden behind the tool shack, making out while her father drank his earnings away. He had felt that memory go, a half-remembered moment that tugged at his heart as it slipped away.*

"Win?" Asin asked, looking at the group.

"I know not, Hero Asin," Omrak said, his brows furrowed. "The monsters we have faced have been varied. I must believe that other parties have faced their own challenges."

"Lost. Twice," Asin said, ears drooping.

"Aye," Omrak agreed.

"The top group hadn't lost anything as of yesterday," Daniel said softly, shaking his head. "I thought if we won all of ours today we might have a chance. But…"

"Salamander. Bad," Asin said. "Right run."

"I know," Daniel's fist clenched as he spoke. "If we have any chance at this, we'll need to win the next fight."

Murmurs of agreement rose from his friends. Friends that he had sacrificed a lot for, memories and experience, his safety. It galled him to think it might be for nothing – but better nothing than a death. Because that, he could not heal.

\*\*\*

"And facing DAO are a tribe of Redskin Orcs!" roared Jules. "As you have seen, these Orcs are aggressive, vicious and most of all, out for blood! They'll trade their lives for the Adventurers. DAO better be ready for a real fight this time!"

"Orcs." Danie's lips curled up, memory returning about the damn monsters they had faced. Of course, those were green-skinned Orcs, creatures who were 'less' savage than the ones they faced now. Redskin Orcs were known to be nomads, monsters that were barred from the Orc states due to a past disagreement. They plagued both nations with their presence - attacking, raiding and otherwise harassing smaller settlements.

"Skills," Asin said with concern, knives held in her hand. "Crossbow."

"Agreed," Daniel said. Unlike before, he had the crossbow in hand and knocked already. This particular crossbow bolt looked different to the others, with a bulbous head that contained a small bottle of liquid inside it. It was one of his last explosive bolts - the other used to deal with the Thyreophora.

"I shall guard us," Omrak said, hunching down as he waited. To cover for the healing of his leg, Omrak had taken more static positions, keeping closer to the team in an effort to deceive the watchers.

As the doors rolled open, Daniel raised his crossbow. Still, he held off shooting until the Orcs were within the arena, knowing that if he purposely damaged the arena, he would have to pay for it later. Almost immediately though, the Redskin Orcs rushed the group, making Daniel pull on the trigger in haste.

The crossbow shifted slightly, not much, but just a little and instead of striking in the center of the group exploded to the side. Luckily, the shift caught one of the seven Redskin Orcs full-on, the potion bottle shattering on impact. In seconds, the Skill-compressed fluid expanded, spreading over the Orc and splattering another near him. On contact with air, the potion also burst into flames, sending the first Orc screaming and rolling while distracting the other unfortunate enemy.

"Damn it," Daniel swore and eyeballed the distance. The Orcs were covering the ground too fast for him to reload and so Daniel tossed the crossbow behind him, grabbing hold of his hammer from its loop in his belt as he strode up to join Omrak.

Asin began tossing her knives out, casting **Piercing Shot** as she targeted a slimmer female Orc behind. A roar, a taunt, forced the trio's eyes to lock onto the massive lead Orc. Unwillingly,

Daniel and Omrak found themselves rushing to the creature, anger and Skill clouding their judgement. Even Asin focused her throws at it, **Piercing Shots** tearing through a hastily raised arm and stomach in quick succession.

"Die!" Omrak howled as he swept his huge sword at the monster. With a contemptuous swing, the Orc blocked the attack, its sneering face growing slightly more serious as their blades clashed and the Orc was stepped back as he dealt with the young Northerner's strength.

"What he said," Daniel snarled as he ducked a swing by another Orc's sword as he **Shield Bashed** the tank Orc back. Before he could recover, his first attacker, sporting dreads and a serrated blade landed a cut across Daniel's shoulder. Glowing red, the attack actually split the metal of Daniel's armour, but luckily the blow had lost most of its strength by the time it reached his flesh. Even then, Daniel found his grip on his hammer opening involuntarily as pain shot down his arm, the strap the only thing stopping it from falling. Still, at least the pain refocused Daniel's mind.

Another slash, this time unpowered came sweeping at Daniel. Stepping backwards, Daniel blocked the attack with his shield even as he cast a **Minor Healing (II)** on himself, the spell re-stitching his wound partly closed and allowing him to grip the hammer handle again.

"**To me!**" Omrak roared, taunting the group with his **Champion of the North** Skill. Forced to attack Omrak, the Orcs turned away from reaching Asin and attacking Daniel, instead focusing their attention on the Northerner. Within seconds, blood began to flow as Omrak was unable to stop all the attacks.

The break, however, gave Asin a moment to recover, a break to charge down and use **Backstab** combined with **Bone splitter** to stun an Orc, dropping the large monster to its knees. Already, Asin crouched over it as she moved to finish it off. Daniel, offered a reprieve, triggered **Double Strike** as well, attacking his own distracted opponent. As the dread-wearing Orc recovered and swung back to Daniel, the Adventurer twisted and struck his shield against a late arrival, this Orc finally having put out the lingering flames from before. Unfortunately, the shield-bashed Orc did not take the bait, instead continuing to focus on Omrak.

A block and riposte by Omrak opened up an opponent's chest, a counterattack that cost Omrak as the tank struck his head with its sword. The Northerner fell back, blood streaming from a deep cut as he waved his sword to ward off the other Orcs. All around the Northerner, a deep red light pulsed, a sure sign of the damage he had received even as blood ran down his legs.

Roaring in Orcish, the tank and his three compatriots rushed Omrak, the giant's blade caught and held by one of the Orcs as the others came to stab him. Instead of flinching, Omrak flashed the monsters a blood-soaked grin as he triggered **the Lightning's Call**, electricity dancing forth from his body to strike all four of his opponents.

Having beaten his own opponent into the ground, Daniel turned a little too late. Caught unaware, clad in iron, Omrak's Skill jumped to him, electrifying the healer and dropping him to the ground. In the corner of Daniel's eye, he saw

Asin hiss in frustration before she jumped onto one of the shocked Orcs.

By the time Daniel recovered, all but one of the Orcs was down – the giant tank. But instead of Omrak facing the red-skinned monstrosity, it was Asin. Omrak was lying on the ground, clutching his chest and turning blue. Casting a **Minor Healing (II)** again on his friend, Daniel pushed himself to his feet, only to see Asin receive a backhand blow across the body that sent her bouncing off the invisible arena walls.

"No…" Daniel sprinted forwards, tucking his head down low as he tackled the monster across its knees just before it swung its blade down. Even then, he heard a scream of pain from Asin before the pair crashed onto the ground together.

Soon, the two were struggling for control, Daniel's smaller and compact body, clad in armor, pressed down upon the larger and stronger Orc. Still, the lessons provided by Angie came in handy, his new meager skills sufficient to stall the Orc from rising to its feet. Strength beat skill however, and Daniel was eventually tossed aside, the giant with one hand on the ground as it searched for its weapon.

Hissing, Asin appeared from behind, plunging her knife into the top of its palm and pinning the monster down. Another knife sought its throat, but the tank punched Asin aside, sending the Catkin sprawling. It was enough time for Daniel to recover, enough time for him to lash out with a **Perin's Blow** and then a combination of other Skills against the trapped monster. Finally, finally, the monster died as Daniel raised his shield to strike again.

With a sigh of relief, Daniel slumped to the ground, exhaustion overtaking him. Too many uses of his Skills wasted without thought in those last few seconds. A foolish move anywhere else but the arena. As Daniel's breathing slowly returned and the thudding of blood in his ears subsided, the Adventurer realised that the waves were roars, roars of approval.

"We won," Omrak said as he limped over, one leg – the wrong leg – dragging behind him from a cut and his hand clutched over his ribs.

"Yes," Asin replied as she struggled to sit-up. Along one arm, a deep cut still bled as she held it close, the blood pooling and dripping from her fingers. With a grimace, Daniel poured more Mana into his healing spells, casting it on Asin first before beckoning the two closer so that he could touch them and cast the **Healer's Mark**.

Once again, Daniel reflected, as they slowly staggered out of the arena to the screams of delight and roars of approval of the crowd, he had managed to escape the majority of the damage. Perhaps they should invest in greater armor for Omrak.

# Chapter 11

"I'm sorry," Jules said once he entered the party's waiting room where the group had returned to pick up their discarded equipment. Too exhausted to carry it for the award ceremony, the trio had discarded their equipment here after repeated assurances of care and a promise to clean and even repair the equipment. It had been too good an offer for the party to decline and so, they had attended the ceremony unarmed and unarmored.

"You were very close. But the other five teams that were ahead of you clinched it. While two are ineligible after today's fights and you were the third," Jules shrugged. "Well, there are only two spots. And both teams have used Major Healing potions to ensure they are completely uninjured. Which, I fear, cannot be said for you." At the last, Jules sent a fixed look at Omrak who flushed under the scrutiny. "Still, you managed the best showing of any Red ranked team. I understand you'll be upgraded the moment you return to the Guild."

"Thank you," Daniel said, doing his best to hide his disappointment. It was not the ringmaster's fault. He just ran the games after all.

Still, missing out on the entrance by such a minor margin stung.

"You can expect a large number of guilds to be after you now," Jules said. "After such a performance, I dare say any of you could join any guild you wish. On very generous terms, in some cases."

"I know," Daniel said, waving the words away.

Jules lips compressed for a moment. "Well, you are welcome to wait a little longer for your equipment, but once it arrives, we'll be grateful if you could vacate the premises. We do have two other tiers to finish."

"Of course," Daniel said. With a few more goodbyes, the ringmaster left the trio to sit in glum silence. A frustrated, glum silence.

\*\*\*

Later that evening, Nicole found the trio of adventurers seated, nursing their drinks with the addition of a new Catkin. The guild mistress sighed, gesturing for Emma and Sara to follow her along. Emma grimaced, but Sara bounced over to give Omrak a consoling hug. Immediately the Northerner brightened visibly at her presence.

"Cheer up," Nicole said, dropping into the seat beside them. "You still got your prizes, didn't you?"

"Fifth place," Asin said, wrinkling her nose and making her whiskers twitch.

"That was your placing," Emma said bitingly. "You were third-in-line to get a spot only because the other two teams were too injured."

"We know," Daniel said, shaking his head. "It's just disappointing."

"Of course, it is. Especially when you decided to showcase your gifts." Emma sniffed. "Cheating healer."

Nicole's eyes narrowed slightly as she noted the way Daniel and Omrak twitched at the mention of the words gifts, but they both recovered almost immediately. It was so quick that she might not have noticed it if she hadn't been looking.

"We weren't the only ones," Daniel said, frowning. "I counted at least seven other teams…"

"Eleven," Nicole said. "There were eleven teams in the third tier that had healers. Of which three were Shamans and Physicians who can speed up but not magically heal."

Daniel nodded at her words while Omrak, seated by the side, had eyes widened in shock. Asin snorted slightly, curling her head into Tevfik's broad chest once again and rubbing her cheek against it.

"It's what we told you before, Daniel," Tevfik growled out softly. "Healer's are rare. Priests are the best, of course, but so few of them are part of an Adventuring order. Those that are available are often added to higher ranking teams immediately."

"Exactly," Nicole said. "It's why you should join a guild. We could add you to our secondary team immediately, and you'd get a chance to visit Artos. Even if you aren't at the right level, I'm sure we can convince them."

"And my party?" Daniel said, glancing at his friends.

"Well, they can't come to Artos, but afterwards you can join them. We'll want to add other members to your team then, but it isn't that big a deal, is it?" Nicole said with a smile. "We have really promising Adventurers including a mage that joined us this year."

"Yours isn't the only guild with great candidates," Tevfik butted in, shooting a glare at Nicole. "We're not a small, insular guild like some. And you already have friends in ours. We'll even let you choose if you want more people on your team. We just ask that you help with some of the serious injuries. The guild master says we can do either a salary or piece work for your aid."

"You'd be a fool to take any of these small guilds," Gadi interrupted the group, hands on his hips. "The Seven Stones is one of the largest guilds in the country. Unlike some, we actually have branches in other cities. That means free or cheap housing, training facilities, discounted purchases with affiliated merchants and smiths and even an emergency fund. Why don't you ask your friends how much they can offer?"

Both Nicole and Tevfik fell silent at Gadi's list of benefits, looking down at the table or away from Daniel. That was answer enough for the young Adventurer. But before he could say another word, a lazy, almost indolent voice interrupted.

"Oh, come now, Gadi. It's not as if the Seven Stones are the biggest guild." The speaker emerged from behind Gadi, who unconsciously stepped aside for the older man. Clad in a vest, a shirt with large, floppy sleeves and tight leather pants, the speaker sported a goatee and a grin as he offered first Asin and then the rest of the team his hand. "Monsieur Labeau. Guild master of the Burning Fields. You might have heard of us."

"Guild master of the Silverstone branch," Gadi muttered.

"Oh, yes, obviously." Labeau shot Gadi a contemptuous glance. "I'm sure Daniel and his friends understood that."

"We did," Daniel said, suddenly finding his throat dry. His friends were little better, their eyes wide as they stared at Labeau and the glowing, enchanted badge on his vest. Even their guild badge was better, more ornate. It was hard to miss talk of the Burning Fields, the largest, most famous guild in Brad. They had more Advanced and Master Class parties than any guild. They had cleared the Necrotic Fungus Dungeon and the Bones Layer, mapping and sussing out the floors to write the definitive guides. They were the guild that hosted the Legendary warrior Hernando Masquez and the mage Cher.

"Well, I must say, I was impressed by your showing. You have guts and some understanding of your Skills. With proper training, support and equipment, I'd expect you to develop quite well," Labeau said. A hand dipped into his pouch, pulling out a small wooden chit in the same design as his badge. "I'd be happy to speak with individuals as gifted as you all. Just show this badge when you arrive."

"Thank you, Hero Labeau," Omrak rumbled, taking the chit and pocketing it. Labeau smiled at them all before turning away to walk out. As he left, the group deflated slightly, the Adventurer's sudden actions leading the group startled.

"Not going to pitch them anymore?" Emma called mockingly to Gadi as he turned away to leave.

"What's the point? The damn Burning Fields are interested. Everyone goes to them," Gadi said and screwed up his face to spit. He stopped when he caught sight of Erin, making sure to swallow carefully. "Just be careful. Big guild like that, someone talented like you gets lost real easy."

"Isn't that our line?" Tevfik said with a half smile as he watched Gadi stomp off. A few moments later, Erin arrived by their table, carrying mugs of ale.

"You've got a lot more visitors, but I have them stalled. Figured you'd want some peace and quiet, but their calling cards are all behind the counter. I'd recommend you start talking to them soon – I run an inn, not a social house," Erin said, smiling.

"Thank you, Erin," Daniel said, echoed soon after by his friends. "We just want to drink in peace. For today at least."

"Well, that, we can help you with," Nicole said, grinning. "Well, a bit. We've all got our own matches soon."

Omrak stared and then made a face, nodding to the guild members. "Our apologies. The matter slipped our mind, but it is true. We wish you the best of luck."

"Thanks, Omrak," Nicole said, echoed soon after by the others. Sara, curled up around Omrak's arm, just giggled slightly.

"A toast then, to future victories!" Tevfik offered, holding out his mug.

"To future victories."

"Victories."

"Hear, hear!"

Daniel smiled slightly as he quaffed his mug and set it down, staring around the table. Perhaps it was not so bad, losing. They had friends, offers and yes, two dungeons still to finish. Perhaps it wasn't so bad after all.

\*\*\*

Later that evening, when the others had left, and the team had returned to the loft to rest, Daniel found Asin staring at him with those large, jade eyes.

"What?"

"Go. Artos," Asin said, pointing at Daniel.

"I'd have to join a Guild," Daniel said, shaking his head. "And that might mean leaving you guys."

"Maybe," Asin said with a shrug and then pointed outside. "Orange team. No healer."

"Ah…" Daniel paused, considering that. It was true. And that team had four others. Perhaps they'd take them on as an addition. Still, something bugged Daniel. "You don't want to join Tevfik?"

Asin froze, her tail even stopped swaying. Slowly, it began again as Asin answered softly. "Nice. But Daniel friend. Gift. Daniel choice."

"That's…" Daniel stopped, suddenly feeling embarrassed at the trust offered to him. "Thank you."

Asin's shrug was all the answer she gave, the Catkin heading for the curtained corner to change. Daniel sighed, lying back down as he pondered her words. With a gesture, Daniel finally took a look at the notifications he had accumulated through the day. The first few were only mildly interesting, skill increases through a wide variety of combat skills. Better shield, mace and combat sense options, better dodging. Frustrated, Daniel twitched his hands as he discarded them all before he found the final notification. As he had expected – he had gained a Level. With a smile, Daniel adjusted his attributes and reviewed his Skills. Next Level, he'd gain another Skill.

Name: Daniel Chai (Advanced Rank Adventurer)

Class: Level 11 Adventurer (02%)

Sub-classes: Level 7 (Miner) (2.5%)

Human (Male)

**Statistics**

Life: 311

Stamina: 311

Mana: 229

**Attributes**

Strength: 29

Agility: 25

Constitution: 31

Intelligence: 24

Willpower: 20

Luck: 16

**Skills**

Unarmed Combat: Level 8 (07/100)

Clubs (Novice): Level 6 (37/100)

Archery: Level 3 (01/100)

Shield (Novice): Level 4 (24/100)

Dodge (Novice): Level 1 (17/100)

Combat Sense (Novice): Level 2 (48/100)

Perception (Novice): Level 2 (19/100)

Mining: Level 7 (78/100)

Healing (Novice): Level 2 (98/100)

Herb Lore: Level 3 (48/100)

Stealth: Level 2 (34/100)

Cooking: Level 4 (13/100)

Singing: Level 2 (14/100)

**Skill Proficiencies**

Double Strike

Shield Bash

Perin's Blow

Find Weakness

Mapping (II)

Inventory (Adventurer Special)

**Spells**

Minor Healing (II)

Healer's Mark (I)

---

**Gifts**

Martyr's Touch—The caster may heal oneself or others by touch and concentration, sacrificing a portion of his life to do so. Cost varies depending on the extent of the injuries healed.

---

Daniel sighed, looking over his gains. It seemed so slow but considering it had only been a few months since they had left Karlak, it was a decent amount of experience. It would unlikely be possible for him to continue this kind of progression – the Dungeon bonus from Peel, the new monsters they fought, were all short-term gains. Now, it would be back to the slow grind. Thinking of the grind, and Artos, Daniel slowly drifted off back to sleep. Perhaps. Perhaps they could find a way in…

# Chapter 12

"You're the healer, aren't you?"

It had taken Daniel half a day to track down the group the next morning. It was not that they were particularly hard to find, just that the city was particularly large. The fact that there were three inns called the Bent Copper had not helped. Daniel was footsore, tired and just a little grumpy after having gone to all three inns in his search for the group, so having the slightly portly leader of the group speak to him like that flared his temper for a moment.

"I am," Daniel said.

Once more, he eyed the group and considered what he knew of them. Gerardo Buchanan was the portly brunette leader, a melee fighter who fought with sword and shield. Like Daniel, he too had an enchanted weapon, but his froze monsters on contact. It was his blade and their ranged fighter – Casey– who had dealt with the Salamanders. Casey's bow was enchanted as well, able to do a variety of enchanted damage but was rumored to cost Mana stones to power. Silently watching the interplay was a swarthy man, dressed in robes with a pair of long, thin swords by his side. Daniel had seen Farhad wield those swords in the arena, leaping and jumping as he struck. It was just too bad that they weren't enchanted, though it seemed that his robes at least were.

Rita was their scout, the team's version of Asin. Of the group, the Helbing was the friendliest, flashing a smile at Daniel as she sat on a raised stool, tiny legs kicking idly. The Helbing was about the size of a human toddler with slightly greater strength and significantly more coordination. While Helbings were uncommon in the general populace – finding living in human and Beastkin built cities uncomfortable – they made a surprisingly large minority among Adventurers. Large at least compared to their population.

"We'll take you," Gerardo said simply. Farhad eyed Daniel with a contemptuous look in his eyes before he turned away to sip on his mulled wine.

"Pardon?"

"You're here to ask for one of our three spaces, right? Maximum party size is seven, maybe eight we're told," Gerado replied.

"Oh. I guess you've had a lot of enquiries?" Daniel said, lips compressed slightly. Damn.

"Many? Just about the entire morning," Rita said, her voice squeakily high. "We've got guilds big and small offering us gold. Heck, even our guild master wanted to reserve the spots."

"Ah…" Daniel made a face at that, realising that of course, their guild would want them to help others out. It was already incredibly generous of them to offer him a place.

"Problem?" Gerardo said, seeing Daniel's expression.

"I was looking to attach my team to yours," Daniel replied before he shook his head. At those words, Farhad turned to look at him again even as Daniel blathered on. "I'm sorry for wasting your time."

"Wait. You're turning down a chance to run Artos? Surely your friends understand?" Casey said, waving his hand. "It's supposed to be chockfull of monsters in there. I hear you can make nearly fifty gold in one run!"

"Fifty? I heard it was more like a hundred," Rita said.

"I think that's for the team," Casey said with a frown.

"I'll still take a hundred for the team," Rita said with a smile. "That's what the Orange and

227

Yellows do on a run now. At that amount, I could even get another enchantment done."

"I know right? I was thinking of a…"

Gerardo rapped on the table to quieten his two friends, rolling his eyes slightly at Daniel. Daniel chuckled, having met and spoken with others like the group. It might even be nice, to have companions who spoke more than a few words at a time.

"I'm sorry, it's not something I can do. We're, well… you know, a team."

"Loyalty is important," Farhad finally spoke, eyes glinting in approval. "In all things."

"Right…" Daniel said, eyeing the Adventurer. "Well, I won't bother you any longer. Thank you for your time."

"Where are you staying?" Gerado said, stopping Daniel before he left.

"The Lonely Candle," Daniel replied automatically.

"Good inn," Gerado replied. Daniel hesitated a moment longer, but seeing no explanation offered for why Gerado asked, he waved goodbye and left. It had been worth the attempt at least.

***

"Hero Daniel! We missed you this morning. Asin and myself, we went to watch the fight in the Arena and collect our reward," Omrak said as he pushed a small pouch over to Daniel. The stocky Adventurer picked up the pouch immediately before slipping it into his own inventory. While the ten gold coins inside was not much of a fortune for an Adventurer, it was still sufficient for others to kill over.

That thought made Daniel snort in amusement. Just over a year ago he had been agonising over saving a single gold coin. And now, he was thinking how ten were insufficient. But, with the requirements for better-enchanted equipment, better protection, payments for repairs and training, it really was low.

"Just wandering the city. I wasn't looking forward to watching other people fight," Daniel said. "Too much time on those sands."

Asin shot Daniel a glance at that, the Catkin having spent sufficient time with him to know how poor an excuse that was, Daniel reflected. She probably also smelt his evasion for all he knew. Omrak however just grinned, happy to take the answer at face value.

"Ah, it was surely a pity," Omrak said. "You missed many great battles."

"Really now? Tell me about it," Daniel said, waving to the tavern wench for an ale and his dinner.

Omrak needed no encouragement, launching into a tale of the battles they had watched and his own grasp of matters. Soon, Daniel found himself regretting missing the action. It seemed that there really was a lot to be learnt from watching.

Perhaps chief among them was the fact that their little party really needed to expand. Many of the tactics that Omrak had learnt while watching could only be counted on to work with more numbers. Almost without fail, any team with a healer had a spell caster in it, with the mages outnumbering healers by a small, but significant, number. At the blue and white levels, nearly a quarter of the teams had spell users of some form.

Teams in the mid-range, the yellow and green certified teams might have a mixture of members, but often mixed their classes more. Each team had at least one, if not more, dedicated ranged fighters. Combined with a spellcaster, they could often inflict significant damage on their enemies before they arrived, breaking up formations and offering their teams an advantage in many encounters.

"Pet Master," Asin interrupted Omrak's enthusiastic recounting of another melee team.

"Oh yes! There was a Pet Master in there. He had a Shadow Cat and a Wilder Boar working for him. It was amazing! The three of them took on half the Skeleton Mob by themselves," Omrak enthused. "They did almost as well as the lead team because of him. Of course, that uhh…"

"Trapper," Asin supplied.

"He helped a lot too. His Skills to lay out those wire and web traps so quickly was amazing. Held up another quarter of the horde while the rest of his friends smashed the others," Omrak said, shaking his head. "I don't know if they'd be useful in a Dungeon, but I know my village would be honoured to have such a skilled Trapper."

"Questors," Asin said pointedly as an explanation. Daniel nodded, taking her word for it. It made sense, a Pet Master and a Trapper in the wilds with a Ranger would be a deadly combination for wild monsters. Not necessarily the team he would want to bring into a Dungeon – at least, not ones like Karlak or Porthos with their narrow corridors.

"Do you think we need more people?" Daniel asked as the pair finally wound down, their descriptions of the assortment of enchanted weapons and amazing Skills finally ending. Once again, Daniel wished he had been there – arrows that shrieked, spells that grew vines and made sand so loose monsters sank on their first step, a shield that reflected light so brightly it stunned opponents and armor that coated its wearer in ice all sounded incredible.

"It would seem wise. Our party is lacking I fear," Omrak said. "Though you have endeavored to wield your crossbow, it is insufficient for our needs."

Daniel ducked his head at that with a grimace. The weapon was slow, cumbersome and in most cases, only good for a single shot. It was better than nothing and could, if they were lucky, remove a single opponent. But it was insufficient.

"Mage," Asin said, tapping her chest.

"You're a mage?' That obviously didn't make sense to Daniel, but it seemed to be what she was stating.

"No. Want mage," Asin clarified.

"Oh. Don't we all?" Daniel said with a half-smile. But mages were hard to find – nearly as rare as healers.

The look that Asin gave Daniel was filled with pity, the Catkin quietly waiting for the stocky Adventurer to catch up.

"Oh…" Daniel paused. "They'd want to join us because we've got a healer eh?"

Asin nodded happily, but then leaned close and whispered a single word. "Gift."

Daniel sighed as he leaned back. Once again, it came down to his damnable Gift. It was why they had such a small group, why they had not looked for more. Taking on Omrak had been a moment of kindness, letting him know of Daniel's Gift had happened only after weeks of working together. Luckily, it was rare that they truly needed his ability. Perhaps they could do that again.

But starting a relationship, especially one that relied on trust as greatly as theirs did, with a lie – or at least, half-truth – was not a good beginning.

"I think we're going to have to risk it," Daniel said finally, glad that his friends had come to the same conclusion that he had. "Soon enough, we're going to need more help."

With the decision made, the trio fell on the food that had arrived with alacrity. Perhaps soon enough, the trio would be more.

\*\*\*

The Adventurers Guild the next morning was surprisingly quiet. It seemed that the attraction of the tournament continued to keep many of the Adventurers busy. In the silence, Daniel was once again impressed by the sheer size of the building. Even with a significant portion blocked off for the vault and other storage areas, the building was still twice as big as a typical barn. Still, with so few Adventurers coming in, the Clerks were standing around in small groups, taking the rare moment of leisure to gossip and catch up with one another.

"Excuse me?" Daniel said as he approached one of the manned desks where a young Clerk worked on his paperwork.

"Yes?"

"I was wondering where I should go to post about a party opening?"

"Wrong room. It's in the Quest portion. There's a board," the bored voice of the Clerk answered immediately, not even looking up from his paperwork.

"Thank you," Daniel said, turning around and walking off. He took all of three steps before a voice called out.

"Daniel Chai?"

"Yes?" Daniel said, turning to look at the speaker. The older woman, the Clerk's supervisor if Daniel recalled correctly, broke away from the group she had been speaking with.

"The Guild Master wishes to speak with you," the supervisor said. Even Daniel could hear the title in her word.

"Me?" Daniel almost squeaked. While he had interactions with Liev in Karlak, that was Liev and Karlak.

"Yes. Come along." The supervisor turned and walked behind the tables, opening a door and guiding Daniel through the corridor. Curious, Daniel looked around but was mostly disappointed at how bland and boring the corridor was. Beyond the abundance of Mana lights, the corridor looked no different from any other with perhaps more doors at best.

"Sir, Adventurer Chai," the supervisor announced Daniel as they entered the room after being invited in. The Guild Master's room was slightly more interesting, slightly more what Daniel had expected to see in such a fabled place. A plush rug that Daniel realised came from a Dire Bear lay beneath his feet while on the walls were numerous trophies from monsters. The claws of a very large Shadow Cat, the wings of a Hippogriff, the stuffed maw of a MegaCroc. Alongside the back wall next to the window was also a bookcase, one that hummed with power from even this distance. And all around him, Daniel could feel the enchantments that warded and protected this room.

The Guild Master himself was a small man, made smaller with age. A pair of spectacles perched on his large, bulbous nose framed bushy white eyebrows and stringy hair. Yet, even seated, the Guild Master carried a sense of latent violence in his body, one that his studious and elderly nature did little to hide.

"Good. Come in, Adventurer Chai. Or may I call you Daniel?" the Guild Master said as he gestured to the seat across his paper-strewn desk. For the life of Daniel, he could not remember the Guild Master's name – everyone just referred to the man by his title on the few occasions he was even spoken about. For people like Daniel at his level, he might as well be royalty for what he had to do with his life.

"Daniel is fine, sir," Daniel said and took the offered seat.

"Good, good. So, I've got this paper here," the Guild Master muttered, pushing at the stacks for a few minutes before giving up. "Somewhere. A letter asking me to keep an eye on you. Now, that's not uncommon – you would be surprised at how many nobles think I'm here to babysit their precious son or daughter – but imagine my surprise when it comes from a trusted colleague.

237

And it's backed up by the name of an Adventurer of some renown too."

After that, the Guild Master paused, obviously waiting for Daniel to interject. However, uncertain as he was, Daniel could only stay silent. It was obvious that the letter was written by Liev and if he was not wrong, Khy'ra too.

"So, I dug into it. And had my people keep an eye on you. In three weeks, you've been in the dungeon for nearly the entire time," the Guild Master said, tapping his lips. "And then there was that display in the arena."

Again, the silence stretched out, neither party willing to budge. When Daniel still refused to speak, the Guild Master smiled slightly.

"That Gift of yours, it's very powerful." Daniel twitched slightly before stilling his face. Even so, he knew that he had given the game away. Not that the Guild Master probably didn't know about it. After all, there probably was a report somewhere about the healing of the Champion.

"I understand that you have had some bad experiences with the nobility before," the Guild Master said softly, eyes intent.

This time, Daniel could not still his surprise as he blurted. "How did you know?"

"We are the Adventurers Guild, my boy," the Guild Master said with a snort. "There's very little we can't learn. I would be wary too with your experience. And it's no surprise that you'd want to be an Adventurer after that. We do have a degree of autonomy many others don't."

"That's not why I chose to be an Adventurer, sir," Daniel protested. Sure, it had some bearing on his choice, but the dream of seeing the world, challenging himself in Dungeons and defeating monsters, defeating Ba'al's poison, that had been his as a child.

"Mmmm... good. I hate those who run into our arms thinking we'll protect them from their sins. We're Adventurers not cowards," the Guild Master answered. "But that Gift of yours – you know it will be reported higher. The fact that it was kept quiet for so long, it could even be considered treason in certain lights."

"I-"

"Relax. No one is saying it yet." the Guild Master shrugged. "Not as if anyone important has died that you could have saved. But there is going to come a time when that's going to happen. And when your Gift is needed. What will you do then?"

"I've never refused to heal those in need. I just, I don't… I can't be a kept man. Not again," Daniel said, eyes meeting the Guild Master. "I refuse to sit around, waiting on the off chance that someone might injure themselves, refusing to use my Mana or Gift. It's a wasted life…"

"Wasted if you save your king?"

"And if I never have to?" Daniel shot back immediately. "No one can see the future."

"Good enough for me," the Guild Master said abruptly, grinning. He reached into his drawer and pulled out a ring, tossing it over to Daniel.

"What…?"

"It's a signal ring. It isn't active until we need it to be, so it won't interfere with your other enchantments. If you're needed, we can find you with this."

"You're… putting me on a leash?" Daniel said slowly, staring at the ring in his hand.

"Think of it as a way for us to contact you when needed. In turn, we'll pacify those who would want to keep you locked up," the Guild

Master said. "It'd be easier if I understood what the cost of your Gift is though."

"That…" Daniel started and then shrugged his shoulders.

The Guild Master grimaced but let the matter drop, running his hand along the table once more. "One more thing. I'm assigning you two others to your team. A Mage and a Ranger." Daniel's eyes widened, wondering how the Guild Master knew of their plans. At Daniel's reaction, the Guild Master's nostrils flared. "Do you think I came to my position by sitting behind a desk? Any fool can tell what your team needs."

Daniel coughed at that, ducking his head low in embarrassment. Of course, he would know as well, if not better than them, what they needed.

"Good. One last thing. Your team is going into Artos."

"How…?"

"Guild. Master." The old man laughed then waved his hand, clearly dismissing the young Adventurer. Daniel walked out, puzzled and a bit confused, but slowly growing elated. Even if he had failed numerous times, it seemed that they were still going to be able to make it into Artos. Wait till he told his friends.

On that thought, Daniel sped up his steps. If he did not hurry, he would miss the tournament again.

# Author's Note

If you enjoyed reading the book, please do leave a review and rating. Not only is it a big ego boost, it also helps sales and convinces me to write more in the series!

If you enjoyed this, check out my other series:

- Life in the North (An Apocalyptic LitRPG)

https://readerlinks.com/l/729295

- A Gamer's Wish (An Urban Fantasy LitRPG)

https://readerlinks.com/l/729151

- A Thousand Li (a cultivation series inspired by Chinese wuxia and xianxia novels)

https://readerlinks.com/l/729231

For more great information about LitRPG series, check out the Facebook groups:

- Gamelit Society

https://www.facebook.com/groups/LitRPGsociety/

- LitRPG Books

https://www.facebook.com/groups/LitRPG.books/

# About the Author

Tao Wong is an avid fantasy and sci-fi reader who spends his time working and writing in the North of Canada. He's spent way too many years doing martial arts of many forms and having broken himself too often, now spends his time writing about fantasy worlds.

If you'd like to support him directly, Tao now has a Patreon page where previews of all his new books can be found!
https://www.patreon.com/taowong

For updates on the series and the author's other books (and special one-shot stories), please visit his website: http://www.mylifemytao.com

Subscribers to Tao's mailing list will receive exclusive access to short stories in the Thousand Li and System Apocalypse universes:
https://www.subscribepage.com/taowong

Or visit his Facebook Page:
https://www.facebook.com/taowongauthor

# About the Publisher

Starlit Publishing is wholly owned and operated by Tao Wong. It is a science fiction and fantasy publisher focused on the LitRPG & cultivation genres. Their focus is on promoting new, upcoming authors in the genre whose writing challenges the existing stereotypes while giving a rip-roaring good read.

For more information on Starlit Publishing, visit our website!
https://www.starlitpublishing.com/

You can also join Starlit Publishing's mailing list to learn of new, exciting authors and book releases.
https://starlitpublishing.com/newsletter-signup/

# Read an excerpt of Book 5 of Adventures on Brad series:
# The Adventurer's Bond

## Chapter 1

The party of five Adventurers traversed the first level of Porthos - one of Silverstone's three dungeons - carefully, heads swivelling in slow order as they checked their surroundings. The six-foot-wide walkway of stone they walked upon joined one magically-levitated platform to another, crossing empty space at a stomach-churning height. Below, wisps of mist hid and revealed additional platforms and walkways beneath them. On occasion, the screech of an imp or the low chittering sounds of their conversation floated upward to the party.

A stout figure in simple brown and green leather moved at the head of the group, bow held in one hand and a trio of arrows in the other. Occasionally, the figure would stop and crouch low as it stared at the ground before rising and moving forward again with a small wave of their hand. Brown hair, shorn short and rough along the skull, framed a pair of liquid brown eyes, a slightly curved nose and thin lips. A small scar bisected one eyebrow, giving the teenage Ranger a more sinister air.

"We will not clear this floor at this rate," rumbled Omrak, the large blond barbarian from the North, as he walked behind the Ranger, his massive two-handed sword held in hand and resting on his shoulder. Sheathed alongside his enchanted, soft leather tunic was a trio of throwing axes, held in place by a simple leather baldric. Along one tree-trunk sized leg a short sword hung, appearing deceptively small, like a large knife, strapped to his thigh.

The Ranger stiffened slightly before continuing to move at her original slow pace. Daniel rubbed his nose with his shield hand, briefly blocking his view. In his other hand, the rockbow rested lightly, waiting for Daniel to load and fire the specialized weapon as he trudged just behind Omrak. He looked over at the youngster and decided – once again – against requesting the barbarian to speak softer.

"We're here to learn to work together, Omrak, not clear the floor," Daniel consoled the Northerner softly. "I'd rather we learn to do so here than in Artos. At least here we know the dangers."

"A good decision," the Mage who walked directly beside Daniel agreed. He turned sideways, smiling ingratiatingly at Daniel while he waved a ringed hand at their surroundings. Daniel noted once again the surprisingly calloused and scarred pair of hands, a contrast to the refined appearance other Mages often showcased. Dark, glistening hair and a beard adorned the Mage's head, hair once again slicked back by the waving hand after he finished gesturing. "Though our companion's speed is low."

"Trap-finding," Asin, the only Catkin member of the five, said. Her tail waved behind her lazily as she watched the back of the group from her position ten steps behind, her keen senses having picked up the conversation between the trio. Unlike the heavily armed and armored pair, the Catkin had on a light leather brigandine that covered her torso, a short cloak and crisscrossing baldrics of throwing knives across her body. More throwing knives sat on her thighs and upper arms, and a pair of larger knives sat on her hips for close-combat.

"But there is only one type of trap on this floor," said Omrak. "We should be seeking battle!"

"If you don't quieten down, I'm sure we'll find some," the Mage replied with a grimace and turned back to his side of the walkway to scan for trouble.

"I am quiet, Rob," Omrak hissed insistently, even going so far as to turn around to glare at the Mage. Instead, he met Daniel's placid brown eyes.

"Eyes forward, Omrak. You know better," Daniel said. The Northerner flushed but nodded, swinging back around and hurrying to get back into line, eyeing both the empty skies and the misty clouds below. Eventually, the quintet made their way to a larger, more stable platform where Daniel held a hand up, signalling a stop.

"Alright. I think that's enough for now. Thank you, Tula," Daniel said. The Ranger bobbed her head slightly, accepting Daniel's words and making him smile slightly. Tula amused him as the young lady was a happy, outspoken woman outside the dungeon. But inside, she became as quiet and taciturn as Asin. "It looks like your trap detecting abilities are slower than Asin's. Maybe it's because they're more suited for the outdoors. Either way, I'd like to adjust our positioning."

"Finally," Omrak grumbled.

Ignoring the blond, Daniel continued to speak. "Asin, you take the front. Omrak will be behind her, ten feet back. Tula, you and Rob will be in the middle to provide ranged support. I'll take the back."

When he received confirmation from the group about their new formation, Daniel smiled. So far, at least, there had not been any major conflicts of personalities. Luckily, they were all Advanced adventurers and as such, each had some modicum of experience in Dungeons. The idiots, the foolhardy hotheads and those who could not work in teams did not often progress pass Beginner Dungeons.

"Let's rest here for ten minutes, and then we'll try to push for the Floor Champion."

Omrak grinned widely at these words while the others just nodded in affirmation. As the group spread out to watch one corner of the platform each, they reached for their trail rations, pulling from their inventory water and a simple mixtures of nuts, fruits and dried meat. Daniel noted how Tula, while not having the actual Adventurer Class, had a Skill of her own which allowed her to conveniently store her belongings in the small satchel by her side.

"Enchanted holding?" Asin asked, her head cocked curiously to the side when she saw Rob pull his rations from a pendant on his chest.

"Yes," Rob said, touching the pendant. "A gift from my Master." There was a hint of warning in his voice, a sign that avarice towards this item would bring significant consequences from an irate Master Mage.

"Expensive?" Asin said.

"Very much so. Enchanted work like this is in extreme demand because it requires a significant understanding of spatial magic," Rob said. "It is a specialized field and is expensive to develop. More so than other forms of enchanting."

Daniel nodded slowly. He absently wondered if spatial magic was a specialization of a Class which would be made available at Level 20 or if it was just an area of focus. Of course, he did not ask, as Classes could be a touchy subject. The Focused, in particular, were touchy about levels. The Focused were people like Tula who had received and stuck to a single Class since their age of majority, a choice made when their initial 'Minor' Class had been given up. This allowed the Focused to gain significant levels since they were not 'splitting' their experience gain across multiple Classes. It did, however, reduce the variety of Skills they had access to and made it simpler to grasp their strength if their Levels were known. As such, discussing Classes and Skills in detail were anathema to the Focused.

In truth, Daniel considered the Focused the lucky ones – able to choose a profession when they reached their age of majority rather than have one forced upon them like most Farmers, Miners and those of the lower classes. Certainly, there were Focused Miners, but they were more often a case of circumstance than choice. They certainly did not go about flaunting their status. Not that Tula or Rob had. Yet.

Conversation petered out soon after, the quartet chewing and drinking quickly while allowing their bodies to rest. It was Tula who first noticed the incoming horde - a swarm of three-foot-tall, red-skinned creatures with black claws and web-like wings. Tula let out a low cry of warning as she swiftly stood, her bow in hand and an arrow snatched from the ground where it had been stuck point first.

"Two dozen," Tula reported as she squinted. She frowned slightly, spotting a much larger Imp lagging behind the swarm of red-skinned, black-clawed flying monsters. Swiftly, she drew the string to her cheek and fired, grasping a second arrow immediately even as the Ranger activated her first Skill, **Arrow Storm**.

This was the first time Daniel had a chance to observe the Ranger's Skill. **Arrow Storm** created multiple temporary copies from a single arrow which flew in a wide or tight arrangement around the original as desired by its user. With time and experience, Tula would be able to guide those impermanent arrows to their target better, but for now, they flew unguided in a wide formation towards the Imps. Even so, the swarm of imps was forced to take evasive action, flapping their tiny wings as they dodged the incoming projectiles, leaving only a pair injured, one fatally. Still, the attack gave the other Adventurers the break they required.

Rockbow braced against his shoulder, Daniel exhaled before pulling the trigger. The rockbow was a modified crossbow that threw explosive rocks into the air, sending tiny shards flying towards the Imps. The weapon was nothing more than an annoyance to larger creatures but to the smaller Imps with their fragile wings, it could be deadly as Daniel showcased. Already turning aside from the initial attack by Tula, a trio of Imps were caught and bunched tightly together when the Adventurer fired. The crack of the stone flying through the air and the shriek of the Imps accompanied each other as the rocks shred the thin membranes of the creatures' wings. In a second, the trio of monsters were sent spiraling into the abyss below.

With the two dedicated ranged weapons unleashed, the Imps flapped their wings quicker as they wheeled around, lining up to tear into the party. It was then that they met the next layer of the Adventurers' defenses. Firstly, Asin's throwing knives flashed in the pale blue Mana light of the Dungeon, catching the monsters in their chests as they unerringly struck their target. Each knife carried with it a small charge from the Catkin's lightning-enchanted bracers, shocking the monsters, long enough for Omrak to wield his oversized sword to slice apart the distracted monsters as they were gliding in.

Once the remaining Imps made it past Omrak, Daniel was ready with his shield to defend himself and Rob. Rather than drop his rockbow, the Adventurer focused on defense at the moment, hoping to get a second effective shot with the weapon when the Imps passed by.

In addition, star-shaped and pointed enchanted spikes activated around Rob, flying forwards and homing in on the nearest Imps. Even a last-minute jerk from the monsters was too slow, allowing each of the pair of enchanted defenses to tear into and exit the monster's chests. Together, the pair of darts wove their way through the air around the mage. This last defense deterred all but the bravest of monsters, forcing them off. And those which refused to back off were Shield Bashed aside by Daniel.

Monsters which fell to the ground were quickly dispatched by the Adventurers, facing death by knife, sword or boot. Working together, the quintet made short work of the larger than normal swarm of Imps. As the Imps dissolved into blue motes, leaving behind tiny Mana stones, Daniel found himself exhaling with relief. At least no one stabbed anyone else in the back. Literally or figuratively.

"Mine!" Asin growled at Rob who was in the process of storing a few looted Mana stones in a pouch by his side.

"This is a party pouch," Rob said, his back straightening at the Catkin's tone. "I have separated my personal funds from it."

"Actually, we generally let Asin store and track the stones," Daniel said hesitantly.

"That makes no logical sense. If the Catkin were to fall into a trap or her corpse be otherwise irretrievable, we would lose all our earnings," Rob protested. "It is illogical to not split our collection."

"Well, it's what we've done before," Daniel muttered. He grimaced slightly, realising he didn't know how to explain the reason for the rule to Rob. At least without potentially insulting his long-time Catkin friend. After all, he had allowed Asin to collect the stones because she liked doing so. And Omrak had never protested, being the easy-going individual that he was. After that, it just had become habit.

"Traditions are but shackles of the past," Rob said. "I am not convinced on the need for our scout – the most vulnerable member of our party – to be entrusted with the full extent of our earnings."

"Look, let's go with our party rules for now and discuss changes once we are out of the dungeon," Daniel said.

"Very well. My protest is, however, lodged," Rob said before he fished the stones out from his pouch and handed them to Asin. She carefully took them from Rob, staring at the pair carefully before she nodded and slipped them into her own pouch. Asin was so focused on the stones that she missed the pursing of Rob's lips as she stared at the magical objects.

Tula tapped her foot on the ground, the slight noise and motion causing the experienced Adventurers to look over. The woman nodded to the next walkway, before looking expectantly at the others. At their frowns, she pointed to Asin and then the walkway before staring again.

"Oh," Omrak said, loudly proclaiming his sudden enlightenment. "The woman desires us to continue!"

Tula winced at the loud Northerner, shooting the blond giant a glare who smiled obliviously. Daniel winced, catching the byplay, but waved Asin forwards. The Catkin nodded with a sniff and loped over to the next walkway, bending quickly to scan for danger before proceeding forwards at a markedly faster pace than Tula.

Grinning, Omrak followed after Asin after giving her sufficient space in front. The pair of newcomers glanced at one another, sharing a brief second of camaraderie before they too followed, leaving Daniel to follow behind and muse about the new party mix.

\*\*\*

Hours later, the quintet finally found the Floor Champion. Or, in their case, the Imp Overseer found them. A floating walkway a few platforms behind them had connected with their route, creating a sudden and entirely unexpected path to the Adventurers. Descending from a platform above the group, through the newly created walkway, the Floor Champion came from behind, his intimidating, muscular but luckily, grounded presence noted by Daniel before the group was surprised. Still, caught out of position, the Adventurers scrambled to adjust their formation.

Daniel sighted down his rockbow, barely able to send a single shot into the incoming group of Imps which preceded the Floor Champion. Behind him, Tula sent arrow after arrow at the group, reserving her Arrow Storm until the Imps were nearly upon the three at the back and releasing the phantom arrows in a wide barrage. The attack caught many of the Imps by surprise, slaying a few and disrupting others, leaving them prey to Rob's spikes.

Rob hid behind Daniel's larger bulk, crouching low behind the armored Adventurer as he withdrew additional enchanted items from his pouches. Ignoring the smaller Imps, Rob rolled a small ball ahead of the group towards the oncoming Floor Champion. The ball bounced over an unseen rock, nearly dropping off the edge of the walkway before coming to a stop, the black and iron patterned steel ball gleaming in the fitful blue light of dungeon's illumination.

"Erlis's tears, that was close," Rob muttered to himself.

Rob then fished out a second, smaller ball and tossed it forwards after whispering a quick incantation. This ball rolled forwards and deployed after three seconds, exploding in a tiny puff of metal. The shattered iron pieces rapidly began to grow icicles on the ground, spiked and frozen caltrops suddenly appearing on the walkway.

By this time, the majority of the remaining Imps had flown past the group, leaving behind minor cuts and bruises. The out of position Imps now flapped their wings as they attempted to gain height or ducked beneath the walkway to approach the group again. Rather than offer the Imps a respite and the chance to attack at their leisure, Omrak roared, triggering his Skill - the Challenge of the North. The Imps, enraged and drawn by the powerful taunt, stopped angling for position and winged towards Omrak, intent on ending the Northerner immediately.

Many of those who approached were batted aside, others were pierced by throwing knives cast by Asin as she loped forwards to aid Omrak. With so many attackers on hand, Asin triggered her own multi-weapon ability, Fan of Knives, creating a spray of throwing weapons that delivered shocking results.

"These are ours, Friend Daniel!" Omrak roared, swinging his giant two-handed sword around, his arms beginning to bleed from small cuts. As he accumulated additional injuries, Omrak's rage Skill activated and a slowly increasing red glow surrounded his body.

"Got it!" Daniel called back, answering Omrak without turning around.

As the large Overseer passed the first of Rob's balls, the enchanted trap exploded into action. It unleashed a cloud of tiny spores into the air which the Overseer inhaled. An errant gust of wind brought some of the spores towards the trio, catching Daniel and Tula by surprise. Both managed to stop themselves from inhaling the spores, but almost immediately Daniel's eyes began to water and itch.

"Close your... oh, nevermind," Rob said, having realised what was happening too late. The Enchanter himself had a pair of newly donned goggles covering his own visage.

With a snarl, Daniel cast **Healer's Mark** on himself and then Tula, grateful that the Overseer, in his sudden partial blindness and coughing fit, had stumbled into the caltrop field. As the healing pulse from the spell took effect, Daniel found his eyes itching and watering less. Still, the delay in casting both spells allowed the Overseer to limp close, it's whip swirling around his body to attack.

Rob, seeing his party mates distracted, gestured with his hands, taking direct control of his enchanted weaponry. The spikes flew downwards, one was batted aside by the whip but diverted its trajectory enough to allow Daniel to catch it on his shield. The second shot forwards towards the

Overseer, only to be dodged by a tilt of the Overseer's large body.

"Ba'al's blessing!" Daniel cursed as he dropped the rockbow to the ground and tugged his hammer free. He took a step forwards and then stopped, realising he dared not approach the Overseer across the trapped ground.

"Right," Tula cautioned, her eyes squinted tightly as she loosed an arrow from her recurve bow directly at the Overseer. The arrow gleamed with blue light as the Ranger used her Skill, Penetrating Strike, causing the arrow to fly too fast to be dodged entirely and impaling the Overseer's left shoulder.

With Daniel holding the edge of the trapped zone with his shield and both Rob and Tula harassing the Overseer from a distance, the Floor Boss was forced to duck and dodge attacks in a confined space. Unable to build up momentum across the trapped floor, the Floor Boss was unable to push past Daniel's shield and hammer, suffering from the occasional buzzing strikes of the spikes and the arced **Homing Arrow** shots of Tula that impacted its back. With no recourse, and having had experience fighting the monster before, the group of Adventurers quickly slew the Floor Champion, leaving Asin to pick up the leftover Mana stone and later on, the Floor Chest they found on its original platform.

Their short-term task completed, the group trooped towards the nearest exit – in this case, the entrance towards the second floor and the portal back to the exit at the second floor's entrance. As they traversed back, Daniel could not help but consider the words he would have to speak to his new party members later.

**Continue reading here:**
**https://readerlinks.com/l/729119**

Made in the USA
Las Vegas, NV
18 October 2021

32600138R00156